MICHELLE PEREZ

Michael Martinez

Edited by
Karinne Keithley Syers

Cover Art by
Christine Underwood

Proofreader
Kristina Satter

Page Design by
Meghan Black

I would like to take a moment to thank my former writing professor and mentor, William M. Hoffman. He always believed in me.

Although this story is fiction, some of these events did happen. The names of the people involved in those events have been changed.

1977

The year was 1977. *Star Wars: A New Hope* came out. "Help me, Obi-Wan Kenobi, you're my only hope." Another great movie was *Saturday Night Fever*. "Ya know, I work on my hair a long time and you hit it. He hits my hair." Like most people, I hated disco but something about *Saturday Night Fever* inspired me, inspired me to do what? I don't know. And before *E.T. The Extra Terrestrial* (great movie by the way, I cry every time), there was *Close Encounters of the Third Kind*. "Just close your eyes and hold your breath and everything will turn real pretty."

Also, in 1977, the New York Yankees won the World Series. The Yankees beat the Dodgers in game six. I was more of a Mets fan, though—Darryl Strawberry, Gary Carter, and Keith Hernandez—those were my guys. Also, related to sports, Bruce Jenner—aka Caitlyn Jenner—was on a Wheaties box.

1977 was also a great year for songs. We had "Jamming," by Bob Marley & the Wailers. "Oh, yeah, well, alright. We're jammin'. I want to jam it with you." And there was also "Black Betty," by Ram Jam. "Whoa, Black Betty (bam-ba-lam). Whoa, Black Betty (bam-ba-lam)." And of course, I can't forget "I Feel Love" by Donna Summer. "Ooh it's so good, it's so good. It's so good, it's so good. It's so good."

Another ginormous, stupendous, supercalifragilisticexpialidocious thing that happened in 1977 was I was born. It was a hot summer day on July 13, 1977. My mother, Carmen Iris De La Cruz Perez, had her back on a cold table with her legs up in the air. The time was 9:32 p.m. The place was Lincoln Hospital, located on East 149th Street and Park Ave—aka the South Bronx. I was going to be my mother's first child. In fact, I was going to be my mother's only child. With my mother was my father, Brandon DeJesus Perez. During the labor the doctor tells my mother:

"Push, Mrs. Perez, push."

"Pendejo, I'm pushing."

My mother sure had a way with words. Anyway, my mother is pushing, and pushing, and pushing, and then suddenly at 9:34 p.m., the power goes out. My mother asked:

"¿Qué pasó?"

The doctor walked over to the window; he saw that all the lights in New York City were out, then, he told my mother:

"The power went out. It must be a blackout."

It sure was a blackout. It was the New York City blackout of 1977. Or, as us Puerto Ricans would say, "El gran apagón de 1977." All of New York City was without electricity. And what do people do during a blackout? They loot, vandalize, and burn down buildings, of course. My mother began to panic.

"Ay dios mío! What are we going to do?"

"You'll have to deliver the baby in the dark, Mrs. Perez."

"Are ju crazy?"

In an attempt to help, my father took out his cigarette lighter from his back pocket and flicked it on.

"What are ju trying to do, burn off my toto?"

"I'm just trying to help, Carmen."

"Ju are not helping. Ay dios mío, if I have this baby in the dark, it's going to be a bad omen."

Just then the hospital's emergency generators kicked in, and the lights came back on. It was 9:36 p.m. Fearful that the lights would go out again, my mother pushed like she never pushed before, but in doing so, I popped out at one hundred miles per hour. The doctor couldn't catch me, nor could the nurse that was behind him. However, at the exact moment that I shot out of my mother's vagina (or toto, as she called it), the janitor walked in. Now I know what you're thinking, why on earth did the janitor walk in? Didn't he hear my mother screaming? Shit, the entire South Bronx heard my mother screaming. Apparently, the janitor was deaf. He lost his hearing in an accident. So anyway, as the janitor walked in, he caught me—apparently, he also used to be a high school quarterback—and then he said:

"What a beautiful baby girl."

That's right, I was a girl. OK, OK, OK, so maybe I didn't pop out of my mother's toto at one hundred miles per hour, and maybe a deaf janitor didn't catch me, but you have to admit, it sounds good. But everything else happened. Anyway, after the doctor gave me the once-over he passed me to my mother. I can remember my parents staring endlessly into my eyes. Well, I can't actually remember my parents staring endlessly into my eyes, but that's what my mother said. My father looked at me and then he looked at my mother and said:

"Ay, Carmen, I can't believe you shot that big thing out of your toto."

I weighed seven pounds and two ounces. My mother looked at me and said:

"My beautiful Michelle, Michelle Perez."

Michelle Perez? Wait a minute, don't I get a middle name? Shouldn't my name be Michelle De La Cruz Perez? Or Michelle Iris Perez? Oh my God. I'm gonna be cursed for life. It's like my mother said, it's a bad omen. First there's the blackout, now I don't have a middle name. The world as I know it is coming to an end. Hold on a minute, Michelle, just hold on, cálmese. You're just a baby. You don't know shit about the world. It's be gonna be OK. You're destined for great things.

3

You're gonna be a millionaire, and travel the world, and fight for world peace, and all that other shit. You just watch and see. Little did I know.

My Parents

Who are my parents? I mean, who are they really? Well, my mother is a short but feisty woman. She's five feet five, slim build, with long black hair. She is an attractive woman. She's very religious and somewhat old-fashioned. She's a housewife. When she isn't taking care of me, my father, or the house, she likes to knit, watch TV, and gossip with the women in the building. She also loves to watch novelas, despite the fact that novelas are very melodramatic. Aside from novelas, my mother had a huge crush on Patrick Swayze, so of course she had to watch every movie that Patrick Swayze was in. Every time my mother saw a movie with Patrick Swayze she would say, "Ay, that Patrick Swayze, he's so sexy. I wish jur father would kiss me like that." Of course, my father would cringe every time my mother mentioned Patrick Swayze.

My mother was born in Utuado, Puerto Rico. When my mother was twenty years old, her parents decided to move to New York City, taking her with them. Shortly after arriving in New York City my mother met my father, and in less than two years they were married. Shortly after, they had me. After I was born my mother couldn't conceive again.

My father was born in Ponce, Puerto Rico. He's a handsome man. He is five feet eight, medium build, with wavy black hair, and light brown eyes. I guess you could say he was a simple man. He liked to fish, build toy models, play pool, drink beer, and hang out with his male friends. He was a super so he knew how to fix things. Unlike my mother, he hated novelas. When it came to TV, my father watched sports, the news, and

The Honeymooners. When it came to movies, my father had very low standards, pretty much any movie with fighting and sexy women appealed to him.

When I was five years old, my father rescued me from impending doom. I went to use the bathroom, and after I opened the door I saw a huge water-bug on the toilet seat. I mean this sucker was huge. What's a water-bug, you say? A water-bug is basically a big cockroach—those motherfuckers can fly too. Why do we call them water-bugs? I have no idea, maybe it's a South Bronx thing. Anyway, the water-bug was just chilling on the toilet seat, and I had to pee really badly. I could see its huge antennas moving up and down. I thought to myself, what is it looking for? Is it expecting to find food on the toilet seat? Then the water-bug turned toward me and I screamed.

"Ahhhhhh!"

My father came storming in.

"¿Qué pasó?!"

"It's a water-bug!"

"Ay, nena, eso es na!"

My father swatted the water-bug onto the floor with his bare hand and then he stepped on it. When he stepped on it, it made a loud squishy sound—ewww. Even after my mother cleaned the toilet with Clorox bleach, I still couldn't bring myself to sit on the toilet. I used the porta potty that day. OK, so maybe I exaggerated about the impending doom part.

So apart from my father being a super and a killer of giant insects, he was very friendly, especially to women. I can remember him talking and smiling to women everywhere we went. I don't know what my father said to these women, but they must have liked it because they always smiled or laughed. Anyway, those are my parents. I wonder if the apple falls far from the tree.

645 Prospect

The first time I saw the building 645 Prospect, I was in the backseat of a car. I was six years old. I was awed by how big the building was, despite it only being six stories. The entire building was built with red bricks. It stood out from the other buildings in the neighborhood. The building had a parking lot, a playground, a laundromat, a large room for events, and two stairways: one in the front of the building and one in the back. The playground had a grassy area, cement chairs and tables with checkerboards on them, and a merry-go-round. Children from the building would spin on the merry-go-round as fast as they could until someone flew off. I, myself, never engaged in such mindless activities, but if I did, I guarantee you, I never flew off. Aside from the merry-go-round, the children from the building played football, booties up, and skellzies, just to name a few.

I lived on the top floor (the penthouse) in apartment 615. The hallways in the building were very long and narrow. They were at least fifty feet long, possibly longer. I always found the hallways to be somewhat intimidating. My apartment was the second door to the last.

The rooftop was forbidden territory, so naturally I went to the roof often. You could see the entire neighborhood from the roof. The neighborhood looked peaceful from the roof. I distinctly remember my friends throwing water balloons from the rooftop. Of course, I never did such things.

For some reason, people hardly ever used the back stairways. Something about the back stairways seemed...scary. I smoked my first cigarette in the back stairway, after which I became very light-headed. Apparently, they call that a "buzz."

When I was eight years old, a young man was shot in front of my building in broad daylight. I had gone to the corner store that day, I don't remember why. I couldn't have been gone for more than fifteen minutes. When I arrived at my building I saw the body of the young man on the ground, near the benches. By then the police were there, and the area had been taped off with yellow police tape that said "crime scene" on it. I remember thinking, if I had left just a few minutes later, or if I had arrived home a few minutes earlier, I may have seen the shooting, or perhaps I would have been shot myself. That's when I started to see what was around me: drugs, gangs, and violence.

Street Games

Street games were a big part of my life during the 1980s. Shit, street games were a big part of every kid's life during the 1980s. It was a great way for kids in the neighborhood to bond, stay out of trouble, and stay out of the house. Street games could be played with very little money, or with no money at all, which is helpful when you're a poor kid from the South Bronx. With tennis, you needed a tennis racket, a tennis court, and of course one of those fancy-schmancy tennis balls. Hardly anyone in the South Bronx played tennis, we played handball. With handball, all you needed was a handball (which was very cheap) and a wall. Anyway, here are all the games I played as a child: booties up, slap ball, punch ball, dodgeball, off the wall, jacks, stoop ball, hide and seek, buck buck, tag, skellzies, and stickball. My favorite games were booties up, stickball, and skellzies.

In booties up a group of kids (usually three or four) would stand in front of a wall and bend over, and a player would throw a ball at them. The goal was to hit their butts, hence the name booties up. Obviously, it wasn't a very intellectual game, but it didn't matter because it was fun. I liked the game because it gave me the opportunity to get back at kids I didn't like, kids like Mario Guerrero. I hated Mario Guerrero. He was always mean to me. Every time Mario's fat ass was bent over in front of the wall,

I would throw that ball as hard as I could. In booties up, you're supposed to try to hit everyone's butt, but when Mario was playing, I only aimed at his ass. Payback is a bitch, Mario. One day while playing booties up, I hit Mario's butt like ten times; naturally he complained.

"Hey, Michelle, how come you're only hitting *my* ass?"

"I'm trying to hit other people but your ass is so fat it keeps getting in the way."

Mario didn't like that. I will say this about booties up: it's not fun being on the receiving end. When that ball hits your ass, it hurts.

Then there was stickball. Unlike baseball, where you needed a bat, a ball, and several gloves, with stickball all you needed was a stick and a cheap ball. Stickball is basically baseball, just without an actual bat or gloves. If we couldn't find a stick on the street then someone would take their mother's broom and we'd use that as the stick. We'd just separate the broom from the stick. As for the stickballs, we bought those; they were cheap. However, every now and then no one had money to buy a ball, so on those days we would just walk over to the local sewer drain. That's right, the sewer drain, aka the stickball graveyard. In the South Bronx stickballs didn't go to stickball heaven, they went to the sewer drain. Why did stickballs go to the sewer drain? Well, because we predominantly played stickball on the street and the streets were filled with sewer drains. One day some kids from my neighborhood and I were playing stickball on the street when the ball went in the sewer drain. With us that day was Jerry Lopez. Jerry was tall and skinny. As a result, Jerry had long arms, so I asked him to get the stickball. He hesitated, of course.

"Are you crazy, Michelle? I'm not putting my arm in there. What if a rat bites me?"

"Jerry, Jerry, Jerry, do you see any rats?"
"No."
"Do you hear any rats?"
"No."

"Then what's the problem?"

"Why do I have to put my arm down there?"

"Because you have the longest arms."

"What's in it for me?"

"You get to play stickball."

"I dunno."

"Jerry, we're winning the game but if we don't finish we'll have to forfeit. Don't you wanna win?"

"Of course, I want to win but…"

"But what?"

"I'm scared."

"OK, Jerry, what's it gonna take?"

"I want one of your G.I. Joes."

"My G.I. Joes, which one?"

"Snake Eyes."

"Snake Eyes? No fucking way."

"Then I'm not getting the ball."

"OK, OK, OK. How about…Flint? He's in good condition."

"Spit on it."

So, I spit on my hand, Jerry spit on his, and we shook hands. Jerry pressed his body onto the ground, and he stuck his right arm into the sewer drain. One of the kids in our group said that Jerry's right arm was slightly longer than his left, so we just went with it. Jerry was close to getting the stickball. I gave him directions.

"A little to the left. A little to the right. There, you're right on top of it. Can you feel it?

"Yeah, I feel it."

"Can you grab it?"

"I'm trying, hold on. Got it."

"Good, now bring it up, slowly."

As Jerry was pulling the ball up, he screamed.

"Ouch!"

"What happened?"

9

"Something bit me."

It was a rat. A big fucking one too. From what I could gather, it was six-to-eight inches long. As the blood dripped down from Jerry's hand, he asked me:

"Was it a rat?! Was it a rat?!"

"Umm, yeah, it was a rat."

"I thought you said there weren't any rats?!"

"Well, I said I didn't see any rats at that moment."

"Now what?"

"Now we call your mom."

Jerry's mother was pissed. She took Jerry to the hospital. Jerry needed four stitches on his hand. After everything was said and done, I still gave Jerry my Flint G.I. Joe action figure. Now I know what you're thinking: since it was technically my fault that Jerry got bit, I should have given him my Snake Eyes action figure, but Snake Eyes was like the coolest G.I. Joe ever, so there was no way I was parting with Snake Eyes. However, I'm not heartless. I did feel badly about what happened. So I added Lady Jane. Her and Flint were a couple anyway. I couldn't split them up. I even threw in five Muscles. (Muscles were tiny wrestling figures with weird faces, kinda like Garbage Pail Kids, but not as gross.) As for Jerry, well, his mother never let him play stickball with us again.

Last, but not least, is skellzies. Although some people called it skully or skellies, in my neighborhood, we called it skellzies. Like most street games skellzies cost almost nothing to play. All you needed was drinking caps and chalk, and most of the time we stole the chalk from school. Kids used caps from orange-juice containers, milk containers, and soda bottles. If it was a cap, we used it. So, how was skellzies played? Simple. You take your stolen chalk and draw a large box on the playground or on the sidewalk. Then you draw thirteen smaller boxes within the larger box. Each box is labeled, starting with the number one. The box labeled thirteen is in the middle. The other boxes are in the corners or on the side. The objective of the game is to get your cap into each box, in order, by gently tapping your cap. The player who gets his cap in each box wins. The game needed at least two players, but usually more than two kids played. When it came to caps, we were very creative. Some kids would melt candle wax into their caps, others would melt crayons into their caps, some kids used clay. Shit, one girl even put a touch of cement in her cap; apparently her father drove a cement truck for a living. Why were we so creative in filling our skellzies caps? Because it helped weigh them down; otherwise the caps would just go flying across the board. A heavy cap was also good for hitting other caps off the board. Do you know what made the perfect skellzies cap? Soda bottles. You simply take an empty glass soda bottle and strike the top of the bottle (just below the circular opening) on the edge of the sidewalk a few times until it comes off. You have to strike it gently, otherwise the bottle will break. Essentially, it looks like a glass ring, a very cheap ring. For reasons unknown to me, it is very effective in coasting across skellzies boards.

Saturday-Morning Cartoons

I'm not a morning a person. In fact, I hate mornings, always have, always will. Even as a child I would always go to bed late. But when it came to Saturday-morning cartoons, I made sure my ass was up at 6:00 a.m. I watched shows like *G.I. Joe*, *He-Man*, *She-Ra*, *Inspector Gadget*, *Transformers*, and *Jem*. My top three were *ThunderCats*, *Voltron*, and *Spider-Man and His Amazing Friends*.

ThunderCats premiered in 1985. The story was about a group of cat-like humanoids that had to flee their home planet (Thundera) before it was destroyed. The ThunderCats managed to escape Thundera and safely arrive on a new planet called Third Earth. As you can imagine, the ThunderCats were the protagonists. However, every protagonist needs a good antagonist. For the ThunderCats, the antagonists were Mumm-Ra the ever-living, and the Mutants, which consisted of Slithe, Monkian, and Jackalman. The ThunderCats consisted of Panthro, Cheetara, Tygra, Wilykat, Wilykit, Snarf, and their leader Lion-O. The main objective of Mumm-Ra and his band of Mutants was to steal Lion-O's sword, the mystic Sword of Omens. Of course, they never got it, and if they did, the ThunderCats always got it back. My favorite part of the show was when Lion-O raised up his sword and said, "Thunder, thunder, thunder, ThunderCats, hoooo!" Then a beam of light would shoot out from the sword. At the end of that light would be the ThunderCats symbol. It was basically a beacon so the other ThunderCats would know where to find Lion-O, and that he was in trouble. I loved all the ThunderCats. They were badass, except for Snarf. Snarf was just...cute.

Next up was *Voltron*. *Voltron* premiered in 1984. Voltron consisted of five robot lions that merged to become one giant robot known as Voltron, defender of the universe. Of course, when they formed to become Voltron they couldn't do it quietly. It went something like this: "Ready to form Voltron. Activate interlock! Dynotherms connected! Infracells up! Mega thrusters are go! GO VOLTRON FORCE! Form feet and legs. Form arms and body. And I'll form the head." To this day, I have no idea what a dynotherm or infracell is, but to be honest, it doesn't matter. The pilots were Keith, Hunk, Lance, Sven, and Pidge.

Voltron's enemies consisted of King Zarkon, Prince Lotor, and a witch by the name of Haggar. Haggar always managed to conjure up a giant monster for Voltron to fight, which Voltron would either slice in half or pierce in the heart with his giant sword. What is it with men and swords? It's a major phallus alert.

Last but not least was *Spider-Man and His Amazing Friends*, which premiered in 1981. This show made me a Spider-Man fan for life. Iceman and Firestar were great too, but Spider-Man wasn't a mutant like Iceman and Firestar. Spider-Man got his powers from a radioactive spider. Spider-Man could climb walls, he had super strength, and he could detect danger with his spider sense, and of course, he could swing from building to building using his homemade webbing, how cool is that? Spider-Man, aka Peter Parker, lived with his Aunt May. He was a photographer for the Daily Bugle. For some reason, I felt like I could relate to Spider-Man. Even though he was a superhero he had his fair share of problems. The show inspired me to read the Spider-Man comics. To this day, I have a box full of Spider-Man comics from the seventies, eighties, and nineties. I wonder if they're worth any money?

Television Shows

Another great thing about the eighties was the television. I watched shows like *MacGyver*, *Different Strokes*, *The Dukes of Hazzard*, *Reading Rainbow*, *The Wonder Years*, *V*, and *The Incredible Hulk*. My top three TV shows were *Knight Rider*, *The A-Team*, and *The Honeymooners*.

In *Knight Rider*, the protagonists were Michael Knight and his trusty sidekick, Kit. However, Kit wasn't a person; it was a car, a talking car. Kit had its own personality; it was actually quite snooty. Aside from being able to talk, it was bulletproof, had a turbo booster (which was used often in the show), and it could reach speeds of at least three hundred miles per hour. Michael Knight, played by David Hasselhoff, worked for the Knight Foundation; their goal was to fight injustice wherever it may be.

Aside from the really cool opening music, there was the opening synopsis, which went like this: "Knight Rider, a shadowy flight into the dangerous world of a man who does not exist. Michael Knight, a young loner on a crusade to champion the cause of the innocent, the helpless, the powerless, in a world of criminals who operate above the law." Aren't all criminals operating above the law?

Next up was *The A-Team*. In *The A-Team*, four military fugitives do good deeds for people using their brains, their muscle, and their guns. The A-Team consisted of Hannibal, B.A. Baracus (more commonly known as Mr. T), Faceman, and Murdock.

Hannibal was the leader of the group. Hannibal was known for saying, "I love it when a plan comes together." B.A. Baracus was the mechanic and the muscle of the team. Faceman was the con man and pretty boy of the team. Murdock was the pilot.

Everyone's favorite A-Team character was Mr. T. Mr. T was a muscular black man with a mohawk and a shitload of gold chains, rings, earrings, and bracelets. As you can imagine, he really liked gold. He was well known for saying "I pity the fool," or "Shut up, fool!" or "I'm gonna get you, sucker!" B.A. Baracus was great, but he wasn't my favorite. My favorite was Murdock. Aside from being crazy, he was funny. Also, his interactions with B.A were great. Together they were like Abbott and Costello, Laurel and Hardy, Bert and Ernie—well maybe not Bert and Ernie. Anyway, the point is they were great together. The best part of the show was when they were trapped somewhere, and they had to build something out of nothing in order to escape and fight their way out.

Last up was *The Honeymooners*. Now, *The Honeymooners* wasn't an eighties show, it was actually from the fifties. One day I walked into the living room while my father was watching TV.

"Dad, what's that?"

"It's *The Honeymooners*."

"Why is it in black and white?"

"It's from the 1950s. Back then TVs didn't have color."

"No color?"

"Nope."

I was shocked. How could you watch a TV show or a movie without color? I asked my father:

"What's it about?"

"Well, you see that big guy?"

"Yeah?"

"He's the main character. His name is Ralph Kramden. The lady to his right is his wife, Alice Kramden."

"She's pretty."

"She sure is."

"The skinny guy in the middle is Ed Norton. He's the clown of the show. Ed lives upstairs, he's Ralph's best friend, and the lady on the far right is Ed's wife, Trixie Norton."

"What's the show about?"

"Well, Ralph is always scheming."

"Scheming for what?"

"Usually to get money but it depends. The bottom line is that his schemes always fail. The best part of the show is when Ralph gets angry at Alice he says things like, 'One of these days, Alice, one of these days, POW right in the kisser.' Or, 'You're going to the moon, Alice, you're going to the moon.' Or 'Bang zoom.' And whenever he's happy with Alice he says, 'Baby, you're the greatest.'"

After that night, I was hooked. I watched *The Honeymooners* all the time. The show actually covered important social issues, such as inequality among men and women. To this day, I still watch *The Honeymooners*. It never gets old.

Summer

Summer in the South Bronx was hot, really hot. Fortunately for me, my father was the super of the building, which meant my parents didn't have to pay rent, which meant there was money for an air conditioner. But how do you stay cool when you're

15

outside? Well, you have three options: go the beach, go to the city pool, or go to the fire hydrant. The first two options weren't that great. Now if you've ever lived in the Bronx then you've probably been to Orchard Beach at least once in your life. The problem with Orchard Beach is that the water isn't very clean; in fact, it's downright disgusting. It's a great place to go and get a tan, eat good food, play sports, and maybe do a little dancing, but that's it—no swimming.

Next up is the city pool. City pools were cheap to get into, although most kids snuck into the pool. As a result, the pool was always packed, packed with little kids screaming for their mothers, packed with teenage boys trying to pick up teenage girls, and packed with kids peeing in the pool. Of course, the peeing culprits were always the boys.

Last but not least were fire hydrants. So how did we stay cool using fire hydrants? Simple, we just opened them. To open a fire hydrant all you need is a big wrench. Someone in the neighborhood always seemed to have one. Once the fire hydrant was open we all went nuts. The closer you were to the opening, the higher the pressure. We would use spaghetti cans to control the water. The top and bottom of the spaghetti can would be cut open. We would usually take turns holding the can. For a while I could never hold the can because of the pressure of the water, but one day I was able to hold the can. I sprayed everyone that ran by, including motorists. Some motorists would get angry but most welcomed the free car wash. The kids in the neighborhood played by the fire hydrant for hours, that is, until the firemen came and turned off the water. But it was OK because as soon as the firemen left, someone would open the fire hydrant again, and we'd start all over.

Bodega

If you ever lived in a Spanish neighborhood, you went to the local bodega. "Bodega" is the Spanish word for grocery store, but bodegas are so much more than just places to buy food and necessities for the house. Bodegas are where you go to hear the local gossip.

"Lynda, did you hear about Mrs. Ramirez?"

"No, what happened?"

"She had an affair with the mailman."

"Ay, que sucia."

Bodegas are where young kids go to socialize.

"Yo, José, did you see WrestleMania yesterday?"

"Nah, man, my parents were too cheap to pay for the pay-per-view, what happened?"

"Hulk Hogan body-slammed André the Giant."

"No fucking way?"

"Yup."

"That's impossible, André the Giant weighs like five hundred pounds."

"I saw it with my own eyes."

Bodegas are where old men play dominos while seated on milk crates and talk about the old days.

"These kids nowadays don't realize how lucky they are. When I was kid a movie ticket was only one dollar."

"When I was kid a gallon of milk was ninety cents."

"You guys are lucky. When I was a kid I couldn't afford to go to the movies or buy milk."

Bodegas are where kids go to buy cheap candy (aside from candy stores, of course). Candies like Now or Later, Sour Patch Kids, Big League Chewing Gum, Nerds (yes, there was a candy called Nerds), Sugar Daddy, and Big Blow. Now when I say Big Blow, it's not what you think—get your head out of the gutter.

Bodegas are where kids go to play video games. Video games like Mat Mania, Contra, Ms. Pac-man, Kung Fu, Double Dragon, and Galaga. I loved Galaga.

Bodegas are where kids go to buy baseball cards. I admit I had my fair share of baseball cards, but I was more of a Garbage Pail Kid kind of girl. What are Garbage Pail Kid cards? Well, they were cards with cartoon kids on them; however, these kids were gross in a comical way. You have to see them for yourself. My favorite Garbage Pail Kids were Adam Bomb, Unzipped Zack, Snooty Sam, and Ancient Annie.

The one bodega that was an integral part of my life was located on East 152nd Street and Union Avenue. The name of the store was Lisa's. The owner's name was Lisa, unsurprisingly. Lisa was a very, very large woman. She weighed about 350 pounds. Her son weighed about 300 pounds. Every Saturday morning (after my Saturday-morning cartoons were over), my mother would send me down to Lisa's to get orange juice, bacon, eggs, a pound of salami and cheese, and a loaf of Italian bread. God, I loved Italian bread. I always bought the seeded bread. I miss my Spanish bodegas.

Food

If you lived in the South Bronx during the eighties and nineties, there weren't a lot of healthy food options. Shit, there weren't any healthy food options. When it came to take-out, we ate Chinese food, McDonald's, Spanish food, and White Castle. Ah, White Castle, those were the days. The White Castle I frequented was located on East 149th Street and Prospect Avenue. Now it's just a parking lot. When I was a teenager, you could buy a cheeseburger from White Castle for just fifty cents. Of course, no one ever bought just one cheeseburger, unless you were broke that day. Most people bought ten cheeseburgers or the ten-pack, as it was called. The downside was that they were very small. Perhaps that was a good thing. Anyway, I loved White Castle cheeseburgers. I could eat a ten pack all by myself. Nowadays White Castle is only good for one thing: cleaning out your intestines.

Another popular food venue in the South Bronx was Chinese. "Yo, let me get an order of chicken wings and french fries." No one ever said, "May I please have an order of chicken wings and french fries?" Or, at the very least, "Can I have an order of chicken wings and french fries?" When I was eleven years old, my friend April told me that the chicken wings were really cat legs, and since I'm a cat lover I stopped eating Chinese food. Of course, it's not true, but when you're a kid you'll believe anything.

Another favorite was McDonald's. Everyone loves those golden french fries, mmm-mmm. I was practically raised on McDonald's. When I was a little kid my father always took me to McDonald's. I always got the same thing: cheeseburger, french fries, and a small Coke, the standard Happy Meal package. The best part of the Happy Meal was the toy. During my teenage years, I purchased a Happy Meal every now and then; it made me feel like a kid again. I would tell the cashier that it was for my little cousin, you know, to avoid suspicion. Anyway, during my first year of college one of my artsy-fartsy friends did an experiment involving fast food. She took a burger from McDonald's, Wendy's, and Burger King, and placed all three of the burgers in an airtight jar for one year. After a year, do you know what happened to all three burgers? Absolutely nothing. The burgers didn't decompose at all—gross. After that I stopped eating fast food.

Technology

Technology sure has improved over the years. When I was a kid we didn't have Netflix, Hulu, or iTunes. If you wanted to watch a movie you had to go to the local video store(such as Blockbuster) and rent a VHS tape. What's a VHS tape? Oh man, now I really feel old. A VHS tape was rectangular in shape and it measured about seven inches by four inches.

When I was kid, we didn't have CDs, we had cassette tapes. Like VHS tapes, cassette tapes were also rectangular in shape, and they measured about four inches by two inches. Very often your cassette tape would get tangled, and you would have to use a pencil to untangle it. Aside from cassette tapes we would also listen to music on vinyl records. A vinyl record is circular in shape and about ten inches in diameter. You place the record on a record player, place a needle on the record, and music would play. Primitive, I know. If you think vinyl records and cassette tapes are bad, you should have seen 8 track tapes—oh man.

When I was a kid we didn't have iPods; we had Walkmans. Before Walkmans we didn't have anything—unless you count boom boxes. Boom boxes were big portable stereos. Just imagine a young man walking down the streets of the South Bronx, carrying a boom box on his shoulder, blasting music. Ah, those were the days, boom boxes and breakdancing.

When I was a kid we didn't have Xbox or PlayStation. We had Atari. After Atari we had Nintendo, and after Nintendo came Super Nintendo. I remember blowing air into my Nintendo cartridge to get the dust out—good times. My favorite Nintendo game was Zelda. I almost finished the game and found the princess but my stupid cousin erased my game while I was in the bathroom. After that I was like, fuck this, I'm not starting from scratch.

When I was a kid we didn't have cell phones; we used pay phones. If you wanted to play stick ball with your friend, you simply called his name from downstairs. "Yo, Hugo! Yo, Hugo, come downstairs!" Nowadays it's almost impossible to find a pay phone. We also didn't have phones with buttons, nor did we have cordless phones; we had rotary phones. With a rotary phone the handle was connected to the body of the phone by a cord. The longer the cord, the further you could be from the body of the phone. As for the buttons, well, there weren't any. If you wanted to dial a phone number, you had to stick your finger in a hole (known as the rotary dial), and then move the dial in a circular motion to the opposite side of the phone. Underneath the rotary dial were numbers, and if you messed up you had to start all over again. After rotary phones came phones with buttons, answering machines, and cordless phones. I can still remember my first cordless phone. I could now talk freely in my bedroom.

Also related to communication was pagers. I'll admit it, I did have a pager in high school. Certain numbers would spell words, but you usually had to look at numbers upside down, for example: 07734 spelled "hello" and 14 spelled "hi." I guess it was equivalent to today's texting.

When I was a kid we didn't have the internet or Siri, so if you wanted to learn something you had to go to the library and borrow an actual book. And when I finally did get a computer, the internet was slow as shit. My internet carrier was AOL, and every time I logged on to AOL it made this annoying sound, like a dial tone, a fax machine, and a car screeching all rolled up into one. And my computer was soooo bulky, not like the thin and light computers of today. And, no, we did not have iPads. God, how did we survive?

When I was a kid we didn't have smart TVs, plasma TVs, or curved TVs. We had big bulky TVs that took up the entire living room, unless you had a small TV of course, which were still bulky, just smaller.

Yeah, technology sure has changed over the years. I still prefer to listen to music on vinyl records though.

AIDS

During the 1980s AIDS swept through the world like a plague; in fact, it was a plague. The first case of AIDS in the United States was in 1981 in San Francisco. Soon after, New York City followed. When AIDS first hit the streets, no one knew what it was. At first it was believed to be a "gay only" disease. But as time progressed people learned the truth. The truth was that AIDS can affect anyone—it's a human disease. I first learned about AIDS when I was eight years old. I overheard my mother talking to her sister about her son, Carlos.

"Carmen, there's something I need to tell you."

"What is it?"

"It's about Carlos."

"Is he OK?"

"He has AIDS."

"AIDS? Are ju sure?"

"Yes, I'm sure."

"How did he get AIDS?"

"How do you think he got it—he's a faggot."

"So now what?"

"I threw him out."

"Isabella, he's jur son."

"He's no son of mine. I can't allow him to stay in my house—not while he has AIDS."

"So where is Carlos now?"

"With a friend."

"Give me the address. I want to see him."

I didn't know what AIDS was. We didn't talk about AIDS in school. So I asked my dad about AIDS.

"Dad."

"Yes."

"What's AIDS?"

"AIDS is something faggots and crackheads get."

"Uh, OK. Thanks, Dad."

Suffice to say, my dad wasn't much help. So I asked my mother if I could go see Carlos with her. She scolded me for eavesdropping but eventually she said yes. A few days later my mother and I went to go see Carlos at his friend's house.

"Titi Carmen, it's so good to see you."

Carlos went to give my mother a hug, but she stopped him.

"I just came by to see how ju're doing."

"Oh OK. Well, I'm OK, all things considering. Hey, Michelle, how are you?"

"I'm OK."

"So would you ladies like anything to drink?"

"No, thank ju. Carlos, we can't stay long. I just wanted to stop by to see if ju needed anything?"

"You mean since Mom threw me out?"

"Jur mother is just scared."

"Why is she scared? I'm the one who's gonna die."

"I'm sorry for that."

"Don't be. It's my fault, right? It's my fault for being a sinner."

"It's not too late to ask for forgiveness."

"I was being sarcastic, Titi. If I'm gonna die then I'm gonna go out with a bang."

"Well, that's jur choice. We have to get going. Carlos, if ju need anything, call me."

"Thank you. Bye, Michelle."

"Bye."

I wasn't happy with the way Carlos was being treated. He was our family, our blood, yet we abandoned him. Well, my mother didn't totally abandon him, but she wouldn't even let Carlos hug her, as though he would infect her or something. So I memorized the address and the next day I went to see Carlos.

"Michelle, what are you doing here?"

"I came to see you."

23

"Does your mother know that you're here?"

"No."

"Michelle, if your mother found—"

"What's AIDS?"

"No one has ever spoken to you about AIDS?"

"Papi said only faggots and crackheads get AIDS."

"Words of wisdom from a typical Puerto Rican machismo male. Well, your brilliantly intellectual father is wrong—and he's an asshole. Sorry, mamita."

"It's OK, Papi can be an asshole sometimes."

"And as for AIDS, well it's a long story."

"So what's the short version?"

"The short version is that AIDS kills you."

"How does it kill you?"

"It attacks your immune system. Most people die from pneumonia or pneumocystis pneumonia, also known as PCP."

"What's pneumonia?"

"Pneumonia is an infection in the lungs. You know, kinda like when you have a cold but it's much, much worse."

"I hate colds."

"Don't we all. But eventually you get better. The problem with AIDS is that it attacks your T-cells."

"What are T-cells?"

"They help fight infections in your body."

"How did you get AIDS?"

"I got it from someone else, someone who had AIDS."

"How did they give it to you?"

"Well…me and this other person had se—made love and that's how I got it."

"Is this other person a man?"

"Yes."

"Do only gay people get AIDS?"

"No, AIDS can affect everyone. I didn't get AIDS because I'm gay. I got AIDS because I had unprotected se—lovemaking."

24

"You can just say sex, it's OK."

"Well look at you. So…have you kissed a boy yet?"

"Eww! Yuck!"

"Have you kissed a girl?"

"Carlos!"

"Just asking. So yes, because I had unprotected sex, I contracted AIDS. So, do you have any more questions about AIDS?"

"Lots."

We spent the next few hours talking about AIDS. Did you know that many people with AIDS were discriminated against? They lost their jobs, their families, and their friends. Also, in Kokomo, Indiana, there was a boy by the name of Ryan White; he got AIDS from a blood transfusion. Parents of the school Ryan attended demanded that Ryan be banned from school. They were afraid that Ryan would infect their children. Can you believe that bullshit? They had no idea how AIDS was transmitted. Some parents pulled their children from school. Ryan's parents had to go to court to have him attend school. The court decided in Ryan's favor, but his parents moved out of Kokomo anyway. Ryan White died at age eighteen. Carlos said people are afraid of what they don't understand. As time progressed, Carlos and I became very close. I went to visit him every week, without my parents' knowledge of course. Carlos was a regular person. He was a freshman in college. He was a photography major. When he wasn't in school he was working. He worked at Woolworth on 3rd Avenue in the Bronx. In December of 1985, Carlos got sick.

"Carlos, are you OK?"

"Yeah, it's just a little cough."

"Maybe you should go to the doctor."

"I did, he put me on antibiotics."

"You've been coughing for a while. Maybe you should see the doctor again."

25

"God, you're a pain in the ass, but at least you care. You're the only person in my family who does care."

"So you'll go to the doctor?"

"If it'll shut you up, yes, I'll go."

"You'll go to the doctor tomorrow?"

"Yes, ma'am."

So the following day Carlos went to the doctor, and he was diagnosed with pneumocystis pneumonia or PCP. The doctor wanted to admit Carlos to the hospital, but he refused because it was New Year's Eve. I tried to convince Carlos to go to the hospital, but he wouldn't listen to me.

"Sorry, mamita, but I'm not spending New Year's Eve in the hospital. I intend to party my ass off."

"But you're too sick to go out."

"Just rub some Vicks on my chest and I'll be good. I'll last the night."

And that's exactly what he did, he partied all night. He partied like he was never gonna party again. He was admitted to the hospital on January 2, 1986. One day while I was visiting Carlos he decided to have a talk with me.

"So, mamita, how's school?"

"It's OK. So…are you feeling better?"

"No such luck. Michelle…"

"Yes?"

"I don't know how much longer I'll be around, so there are some things I wanna tell you."

"What are you talking about? You're going to be fine, you'll get better—you'll see."

"Michelle, I'm dying. That's what this disease does, it kills you."

"No, no, no, you're not dying—you can't die!"

"Michelle, we talked about this. We talked about AIDS."

"Maybe they'll find a cure."

"Maybe they will but in case they don't, I wanna talk to you about some things, OK?"

"OK."

"First: when you become a teenager, watch out for boys. They think with their dicks, they only want one thing."

"What do they want?"

"Well…they want what you have down there. I believe your mother calls it 'toto.'"

"What? Why? That's gross!"

"Trust me, I feel the same way, but something about it drives men crazy, that and big boobs. Anyway, the moral of the story is, when you become a woman don't just give your toto to anyone—and use protection. Second: don't use drugs, drugs like crack, cocaine, and heroin."

"What about pot?"

"Pot's OK, but too much pot kills your brain cells—and how do you know about pot?"

"I hear things."

"Yeah, I bet you do. Lastly, do what makes you happy."

"What do you mean?"

"Most people don't follow their heart, they don't follow their passion. They do what their parents want them to do, or what society wants them to do, in order to conform to norms of society."

"Like what?"

"Like getting married, having a bunch of kids, going to family barbecues, and shit like that."

"What's wrong with that?"

"Nothing, if that's what makes you happy. Do you understand everything I just told you, Michelle?"

"I think so."

While in the hospital, Carlos's condition continued to deteriorate. Carlos lost so much weight I could almost see his ribcage. He had no color. He was ghostly white. His skin was so dry it was practically peeling off. He also had lesions all over his body. The lesions were called Kaposi's sarcoma. Every time I went to go see him I had to wear a mask, not just for my protection, but for his. His T-cell count was very low. In the early and mid-eighties there was no treatment for AIDS. All the hospital could do was make him comfortable. Some AIDS patients were on a trial drug called AZT. The drug had several side effects, but it gave AIDS patients a glimmer of hope. It prolonged their life, for a time. While Carlos was in the hospital he tried to be placed on the trial, but he was denied. Between the PCP, the chronic pain, and the wasting away of his body, he begged for death, and one day he got it.

On March 2, 1986, my cousin Carlos Perez died of AIDS, with myself and his friends at his side. My mother came to the wake along with a few other family members, but because of his sexual preference Carlos's mother didn't come to the wake. She condemned him to die. About two weeks after Carlos died, AZT was approved by the FDA. Great fucking timing.

In 1987, an AIDS group called Act Up was formed. Their goal was to spread awareness about AIDS, and to pressure the government to find a cure and allocate proper funding to AIDS research. They held protests and organized marches. I wanted to do something for Carlos, so one day I went to their office in downtown Manhattan. When I arrived there, a middle-aged man with glasses approached me.

"Can I help you, young lady?"

"Yes, I heard that you have marches for AIDS victims?"

"Yes, we do."

"Well…I was wondering if I could march with you?"

"Do your parents know that you're here?"

"No."

"You can't march without your parents' permission."

"Please mister, my cousin Carlos died last year from AIDS. I just wanna do something to remember him by—to honor his memory."

"I can understand that, but shouldn't your parents know that you're here?"

"My family turned their backs on Carlos when they found out he had AIDS. My mother tried to help a little but it wasn't enough."

"I see. Well, we're marching tomorrow. I'll let you march with us on one condition."

"What's that?"

"That you stay by my side the entire time so I can watch over you. Is that a deal?"

"Deal."

So we shook hands and the next day I marched with Act Up. I'm sure it was just my imagination, but I felt like Carlos was with me that day, watching over me.

Church

As a child, I hated church. It was soooo boring. You sit down in a place surrounded by a bunch of religious stiffs that are too afraid to do anything because they're afraid they're gonna burn in hell, and the ones that aren't stiffs are hypocrites. Take Rosita Morales from 163rd and Longwood; she went to church every Sunday. She always praised the Lord Jesus Christ. Yet she was fucking every José, Juan, and Pedro that gave her the time of day. Meanwhile, she was a married woman. Rosita was forty-seven but she looked younger. She was an attractive woman, I'll give her that. Her husband, on the other hand, was sixty-five and the rumor was that he couldn't get it up anymore. I understand we all have needs, but don't be a hypocrite—just divorce the guy. And then there was the church ceremony; I had to sit there for an entire hour and listen to some guy talk about God and religion. I didn't have to go to church for that, my mother talked about God and religion all the time. Anyway, I never had any love for church, but after 1987 I hated church.

The year was 1987—Easter Sunday. After the ceremony my mother decided to stay and help everyone at the church take down the Easter decorations. She forced me to help. Thirty minutes into putting away the decorations, we ran out of boxes. Sister Mary asked me to go down to the basement to get some more. I didn't know where the basement was, so Eddie offered to show me. Eddie was the church's unofficial super. He helped them fix things. He was very handy. He was five feet six, moderately overweight, with short hair. He wasn't very good-looking but everyone liked him. So me and Eddie went down to the basement to get more boxes.

"So Michelle, what do you want to be when you grow up?"

"I don't know."

"Do you like helping people?"

"Yeah, I guess."

"Maybe you could be a psychologist?"

"A shrink?"

"Yes."

"Eh, I dunno."

"How about a doctor?"

"Nah, I don't like blood."

Then Eddie sat down and looked at me for a moment. For some reason, I began to feel uncomfortable. My first instinct was to leave, but I didn't want to overreact. Plus, I figured, what could happen to me inside a church basement with my mother and everyone else upstairs? Then Eddie slowly unzipped his pants. I asked him:

"What are you doing?"

"You said you wanted to help people, right?"

"Yeah."

"So help me."

He took out his penis and quickly grabbed my wrist. He pulled me closer to him. I didn't know what to say. I didn't know what to do. It was like I was frozen in time. Then he placed my hand on his penis. I screamed.

30

"No!"

Then I pulled myself away and ran upstairs. Eddie yelled.

"Michelle!"

I ran straight to my mother.

"Mom, I wanna go home."

"Why?"

"I don't feel good. My stomach hurts—and I have diarrhea."

"I told ju, stop eating all that junk food. Ven, we'll take a cab home."

As soon as I got home I ran straight to the bathroom, took off my clothes, turned on the water and took a shower. The water was almost scalding hot. I felt so dirty. I stayed in the shower for almost an hour. My mother knocked on the door.

"Michelle, are ju OK?"

"I'm fine, Mom."

"Well hurry up, tengo que mear."

"OK, Mom, I'll be right out."

After I left the shower I went straight to my bedroom. I thought about what happened. Although the actual act only lasted for a second, it felt like an eternity. I felt ashamed. I felt like it was somehow my fault. I didn't tell my parents. I didn't want to tell anyone. I just wanted to forget about it. So that's what I did. I forgot about it.

My Bully

Her name was Jessica Hernandez, and she was my bully. I was in sixth grade, and she was in the seventh grade. She was a bit taller than me and she was fat, really fat. One day while I was walking to class she bumped into me.

"Ouch, watch it."

"What are you gonna do about it?"

As she stared me down, I stood there quietly. I was intimidated. After a moment she resumed walking to her class. And that's how the bullying started. Every week the bullying got worse and more creative. One week I got the ultimate wedgie. Have you ever had an ultimate wedgie? Well, trust me, it's not fun. Eventually I told my Home Room teacher, Mrs. Mahler. Mrs. Mahler spoke to Jessica and I had peace...for about a week. When the bullying started again, I told Mrs. Mahler a second time. This time Mrs. Mahler told the principal. The principal suspended Jessica for a few days, and again I would have peace, or so I thought. When Jessica returned from her suspension she approached me.

"Why did you tell the principal on me?"

"I didn't tell the principal. I told Mrs. Mahler, and she told the principal."

"Same shit."

"Why can't you just leave me alone?"

"Because I don't like you."

"Why, what did I ever do to you?"

"You were born."

Then she shoved me into the wall so hard I thought I was gonna go through it. After that I decided it was time to tell my parents.

"Mom, this girl at school is bullying me."

"What do ju mean, bullying you?"

"Well, she pushed me and stuff."

"Did ju tell jur teacher?"

"Yes."

"Did she do anything about it?"

"She told the principal, and the principal suspended her for a few days, but now she's back and she's bullying me again."

"Don't worry, Michelle, I'll fix that puta. Tomorrow I'm going to school with ju, and we're going to get this straightened out."

"Should I fight back?"

"No. Fighting is never the answer."

"But you just called her a puta."

"Watch jur mouth, Michelle! Saying bad words and doing bad things are very different."

Then my mother left to start cooking. After my mother left, my father spoke to me.

"Michelle, if someone hits you, you hit them back."

"But Mommy said——"

"Ssh. Don't worry about what Mommy said."

"But I don't know how to fight."

"Don't worry, I'll teach you."

"You know how to fight?"

"Of course I know how to fight. When you grow up poor in Puerto Rico, you have to know how to fight. Meet me in the basement tomorrow after school. I have a punching bag there."

The following day after school I ran to the basement and began my boxing lessons. My dad taught me some basic boxing punches: high cross, low cross, high jab, low jab, left hook, right hook, left uppercut, right uppercut, left body hook, right body hook, and finally the haymaker. After the lesson was over my father said:

"I wanna show you a movie."

"What's it about?"

"Boxing."

"What's the name of the movie?"

"*Rocky.*"

After I saw *Rocky* I felt so inspired. I had the eye of the tiger. I even trained like Rocky. I jogged in the street, did push-ups and sit-ups, ran up steps, and I even tried to hit some meat at the local meat market.

"Yo, Juan, you got any meat I can hit?"

"Ah, get the fuck outta here."

Suffice to say that was a "no." Two weeks later I was ready to face off with that bully bitch Jessica. I saw her at school on a Monday. As usual she bumped into me as I was putting my books in my locker.

"Watch it!"

"What did you say, toothpick?"

"I said, watch it!"

"When did you get a backbone?"

Jessica pushed me. I pushed her back. Jessica pulled back her arm and fist as though she was going to hit me, but just then Mrs. Santos, the science teacher, stepped in.

"Hey, hey, hey, what's going on here?"

"Nothing Mrs. Santos. Me and Michelle just had a little misunderstanding. Isn't that right, Michelle?"

"Yeah, that's right."

"All right, get to class—both of you."

Before Jessica went on her merry way, she whispered to me.

"I'll see you after school, toothpick, three o'clock."

"I'll be there."

It was official; me and Jessica were gonna rumble. I was ready. So three o'clock came and me and Jessica met in the school-yard. Of course the entire school was there; who doesn't wanna see a good ass-whipping? Jessica raised her hands and took her fighting stance. I did the same. She took a swing at me. She missed me. She was strong but slow. I had the advantage. She swung at me a few more times, but she couldn't hit me. Finally, I made my move. I hit her in the stomach with a low jab. Then a low cross. Then again with a low jab. Another low cross. But my punches were having no effect on her. I would punch her, and my fist would get sucked into her stomach, like when the X-Men fought the Blob in X-Men 3 (1964). Then I decided it was time for a power punch. I waited for the right moment then I hit her with a right uppercut. She was dazed but she didn't fall. I went for the haymaker but the bitch caught it. She caught my fist and starting crushing it like when Spider-Man was fighting the kingpin in The Amazing Spider-Man 69 (1969). I was on my

34

knees at Jessica's mercy. I didn't know what to do. All I could do was curse, so I did.

"Let go of me, you stupid, fat Ronald McDonald–eating bitch!"

Just then a miracle happened. She let go of me. Could I have defeated her with my words? After she let go of me, she looked at me for a moment, and then she started crying. I couldn't believe it. Then everyone started laughing at her and calling her names.

"Look at the whale, she's crying."

"Is your mother as fat as you?"

"Jessica's a fat pig, oink, oink, oink."

Jessica began to cry more and more. Soon after, she ran away. She ran all the way home. You know what this means? It means I won. I defeated my bully. I came, I saw, I conquered— oh yeah! The crowd lifted me in the air and cheered, "Hip hip hooray, hip hip hooray, hip hip hooray!" However, despite my victory, I felt bad. You should have seen the look on Jessica's face; it was like I broke her spirit. She looked like she was gonna jump off a bridge or something, and as much as I hated her, I didn't want that on my conscience. Jessica only lived a few blocks away from me, so the following day I went to her apartment building. I walked to the fourth floor, and as I was about to knock on the door I heard a man screaming.

"You stupid fat bitch, I told you, sweep the floor before you mop it."

A few seconds later I heard the door opening, so I ran up the stairs to the fifth floor. A man stormed out of the apartment and went down the stairs. I slowly made my way back down the stairs and made sure the man was out of sight. I knocked on the door. A woman answered. Her left eye was black and blue.

"Who are you?"

"I'm Michelle. I go to school with Jessica, is she here?"

"Wait here."

A moment later Jessica came to the door.

"What are you doing here?"

"I…I just came to check up on you, to make sure you're OK."

"I'm fine—now go."

As Jessica was closing the door I noticed her arm was black and blue. I braced the door with my arm and I asked Jessica:

"What happened to your arm?"

"Nothing…I fell."

"Your dad did that, didn't he?"

"What do you care? You called me a fat bitch at school."

"Actually, I called you a stupid, fat, Ronald McDonald–eating bitch, but that's beside the point—we were fighting, and the only reason we were fighting was because you kept bullying me."

"I was angry."

"Why were you angry at me?"

"I dunno. I just was angry."

"How long has your father being hitting you like that?"

"A long time. He hits my mother too. If my mother overcooks his food, he hits her. If he doesn't like the way I clean, he hits me. When he has a bad day at work, he hits me and my mother."

"Why doesn't your mother do anything about it, like call the cops?"

"I dunno. She's scared, I guess."

I felt sorry for Jessica. Then I grabbed Jessica's hand.

"Come on."

"Where are we going?"

"To my house."

"To your house, for what?"

"You're not staying here anymore."

"But what am I going to tell my mother?"

"I'll talk to her. Mrs. Hernandez."

Mrs. Hernandez came to the doorway.

36

"Yes."

"Jessica is gonna be at my house for a few hours—she may even stay over."

"But Jessica doesn't have any clothes packed."

"It's OK—she can borrow mine. Have a good night, Mrs. Hernandez."

When we arrived at my house I told my parents what happened. My father was pissed. Although my father was the king of machismo, he never laid a hand on me or my mother. He wanted to go to Jessica's house and beat the shit out of her father, but my mother held him back. So my parents called the police. When the police arrived, they spoke to Jessica. After hearing Jessica's story, the police called ACS, the Administration for Children's Services. The police arrested Jessica's father. As for Jessica's mother, ACS felt she wasn't suited to raise a child. Jessica had a grandmother in Brooklyn but she was away visiting family in Puerto Rico. I asked my parents if Jessica could stay with us for a few days. My parents said yes, and ACS was OK with it. During the next two days, I got to know Jessica very well. She was actually a very nice person. We became good friends. When Jessica's grandmother returned from Puerto Rico she went to go live with her. After Jessica went to live with her grandmother, she transferred to a school in Brooklyn, so I didn't see her again. As for Jessica's father, he was released and given one-year probation. One-year probation, can you believe that shit? It would be several years before Jessica's mother finally left her husband. I couldn't figure out why. Why stay with someone who's abusing you? Anyway, as for Jessica, she turned out OK. I heard she even became a police officer.

Divorce

The year was 1989. I was in my room listening and dancing to Paula Abdul's song, "Cold Hearted." "He's a cold-hearted snake, look into his eyes. Uh-oh, he's been telling lies. He's a lover boy at play, he don't play by the rules, uh-oh. Girl don't play the fool, now." Then that's when it started, the yelling.

"¡Hijo de puta! ¡Cabrón!"

"Carmen, she meant nothing to me."

"If she meant nothing to ju, then why did ju sleep with her, twice?"

"I dunno, because I'm stupid."

"That's it, Brandon, I've had enough. I want you out."

"Out? What do you mean out?"

"Out of my house!"

"Your house, isn't this our house?"

"I do all the cooking, cleaning, and washing. I do everything, what do you do?"

"I pay the rent."

"What rent? Ju're the super, we live here for free."

"I pay the bills."

"So because ju pay for the cable, the telephone, and Con Edison, that gives ju the right to sleep with other women?"

"Well, I pay for the groceries too."

"Get out!"

"Carmen, wait, give me another chance."

"Another chance? Another chance? Brandon, how many times have ju cheated on me?"

"I dunno."

"Nine times, Brandon. Ju've cheated on me nine times— that I know of."

"Doesn't the Bible say to forgive your enemies?"

"Yes, after the first time, not after the ninth time."

"Can you really put a number on forgiveness?"

"Jes! Or perhaps I should wait until ju cheat on me ten times."

After that there was quiet for a minute. Then my father started putting his clothes in a duffel bag. Before my dad left the apartment, I stopped him.

"Dad, where are you going?"

"I'm going to be staying with my brother for a while."

"Are you and Mom getting a divorce?"

"No, no, no. We're just taking a break."

"A break, are you sure?"

"Yes, I'm sure."

"Mom is very upset."

"Give her time."

Before my dad left I hugged him. A year later my parents were officially divorced. As for my mother, she got herself a little job to help pay the bills. My dad kept his job as super, so we didn't have to move out, but whenever we needed something in the house fixed he would only come over when my mother wasn't home. Despite my parents getting divorced, my father always made sure my mother and I had whatever we needed; my father was always there for me. Still, things were better when we were a family. Divorce really sucks.

Homosexuality

To be gay or to not be gay? That is the question. So one day after school my friends Jasmine and Theresa were talking about their boyfriends, and how they let them get to first base. Then they asked me how come I didn't have a boyfriend. I simply said, "I dunno." While most of my girlfriends had boyfriends, I didn't really have an interest in boys. I dunno, I just didn't find them...attractive. Then, one day, it happened. I was in math class—which I hated, by the way—and I dropped my No. 2

pencil. As I leaned over to get it, the girl next to me also leaned over to get it, and our hands touched for a moment. I looked at the girl and she smiled. Then she grabbed my pencil and handed it back to me. I quickly sat back up in my chair and pretended like nothing happened. Then I felt something…something inside my stomach. I didn't know what it was. I looked over at the girl. She was new in school so I didn't know her name. I began to admire her. I began admiring her face, her lips, and small A-sized breasts. I began imagining what it would feel like to caress her soft skin, to feel her lips on my body, to suck her—ho-lee-shit, I'm gay! What am I gonna do? What am I gonna do? I can't tell my friends. I can't tell my mother. My mother—fuck! My mother is gonna kill me. No, first she's gonna beat the shit out of me, then she's gonna kill me. Just take a deep breath, Michelle. Breathe. Breathe. Breathe. OK, so what am I gonna do? You know what—fuck it, whatever happens, happens. Right now, I just wanna keep admiring this girl in my math class. God, she's beautiful.

My Vagina

So after the hand-grazing incident at school, I'd started to think about my sexuality, my body, and lastly, my vagina. I was thirteen years old, and I'd just realized that I'd never seen my vagina. So I decided that it was time to meet my vagina face-to-face. It was a Wednesday night. I had just taken a shower. I stepped out of the shower, grabbed a small mirror, put my back against the door, opened my legs, and I placed the mirror in between my legs. At first I couldn't see anything. I tried maneuvering my body and readjusting the mirror and still—nothing. Then after a few minutes I finally saw something, but it was so small. Then I told myself, "I need a bigger mirror." So I put the small mirror away, grabbed a bigger one, and I started the search again. For some reason it felt like I was looking for a needle in a haystack, but soon enough there it was—voila. But it was closed, I couldn't see anything. Meanwhile my mother started banging on the door.

"Avanzá, me quiero bañar antes de que comience mi novela."

Shit! Now what? I was gonna have to go in there and open that bad boy up, but I was scared. Aside from washing my vagina, I never really touched my vagina, but I was determined to see it. So after a few minutes of deliberation, I told myself, it's now or never. So I took a deep breath, checked my mirror placement, and I went in. After I opened it, I just stared at it for a few minutes. I guess I was in a daze. I was trying to figure out what it looked like. I was trying to compare it to something—then it hit me. You know what? It kinda looks like a sliced papaya—without the seeds of course. And that was the first time I saw my vagina.

Playboy, Part One

So after I discovered my vagina, I discovered Playboy. The year was 1990, and my mother went to go visit her sister, and she dragged me with her. As my mother and my aunt discussed meaningless gossip over Spanish coffee, I ventured throughout the apartment on a cold day in February. My aunt was married with three kids, but neither her husband nor my cousins were home at the time. My cousins were a few years older than me. All the rooms were unlocked, and except for some loose change (which I pocketed, of course), I didn't find anything interesting. At least not until I reached my aunt's room. After fiercely searching for about five minutes, I found something under the mattress. It was a Playboy magazine. It had to belong to Titi Lynda's husband. At first I wondered to myself, why would Titi Lynda's husband have a Playboy magazine under the bed when he's a married man? Then it dawned on me, Titi Lynda isn't a very attractive woman, especially after she popped out three kids, two of which were very fat babies. Anyway, I saw the half-naked woman on the front cover, and I became aroused. I quickly flipped through the magazine and began drooling over all the naked women. I wanted to touch myself, but I was afraid that my mother or Titi Lynda would catch me. Just then my mother called me.

"Michelle, we're leaving."

"Be right there, Mother."

I quickly rolled up the Playboy magazine and stuffed it in my jeans. I frantically fixed Titi Lynda's bed and then I left.

Playboy, Part Two

When I arrived home later that day, I immediately ran to my room, closed the door, and locked it. I couldn't have my mother barging in. I took out the Playboy magazine, stared at the cover for a moment, and then I opened it. I looked at each page with adoration and lust. I memorized each woman's face and body as though the world was ending. I began to touch myself. First I touched my breasts, then I touched the outside of my vagina. As I was looking through the Playboy magazine I found the centerfold page, three pages that combined to form a poster, a poster of a large naked woman. It was Pamela Anderson from Baywatch, completely and utterly naked. Her skin looked so soft. Her breasts were perfect—despite the fact that they were fake, but whatever, I didn't care. And last but not least was her vagina. I could only see the outside of her vagina, but I wasn't complaining. As with the pencil incident, I felt something inside me, but this time it was a hundred times stronger. Then I touched the inside of my vagina. As far as masturbation goes I didn't really know how it worked, but in my sex education class I learned that the clitoris plays a major part in sexual arousal, so I decided to start there. So after about ten minutes of masturbating my body became very tense, then I felt something gush out of my vagina, but I was too busy having a seizure to notice. Obviously, I wasn't having a real seizure, but my body was convulsing like crazy. After my body stopped convulsing, I felt this sensation that can only be described in one word: "Ahhh." Now "ahhh" isn't really a word, but if you've ever had an orgasm before then you know what I mean. After I was done I sat up and that's when I saw it, there was fluid all over my bed below my vagina. "What the fuck is that?!" I said to myself. I started to freak out. I thought I was dying or something. Later I learned that it was called female ejaculation fluid—who knew. So on February 22, in the year 1990, while in my bed, located at 645 Prospect Avenue, I masturbated to the centerfold page of Pamela Anderson. Then, my mother knocked on the door.

"Michelle."

"Uh, just a minute."

My mother turned the door knob.

"Michelle, why is the door locked?"

"Umm, I'm cleaning my room."

"¡Abre la puerta!

I jumped out of bed, put my pajamas on, threw my underwear and bedsheet in the hamper, and flung the Playboy magazine out the window. Then I quickly sprayed my room with an air freshener. I didn't smell anything but just in case, you never know. My mother started banging on the door.

"Michelle!"

"I'm coming, Mom."

I opened the door.

"Hey, Mom."

"Ay madre, what took ju so long to open the door?"

"Sorry, Mom."

"Were ju doing drugs?"

"Mom, do I look like I was doing drugs?"

"I dunno, jur face is glowing."

"I'm fine, Mom. Did you need something?"

"Just jur opinion. I was thinking of cooking lasagna tonight, what do ju think?"

"Lasagna?"

"Jes."

"Lasagna sounds great, Mom, just great."

"OK. When you're done cleaning your room, help me in the kitchen."

"Sure, Mom."

So that was the first time I masturbated, and it certainly wasn't the last.

Halloween

Halloween for a child in the South Bronx was great. I would dress up as Wonder Woman, Cheetara, or Lady Jayne and knock on doors with my father and a group of kids, asking for candy. Sometimes we got money, mostly pennies and nickels, although every now and then we would get quarters. I know what you're thinking, whoop-de-doo, a quarter, but in the eighties you could do a lot with a quarter. You could use it to play video games, buy candy, or make a phone call on a public pay phone. Nowadays most video games are a dollar. Candy ain't cheap either. And as for pay phones, well they're pretty much nonexistent. Anyway, after I was done trick-or-treating, I would go back home and sort out my goodies. I usually had enough candy to last me the week. Yup, good times.

Now Halloween as a teenager in the South Bronx was not fun. Why wasn't it fun? Well, because of eggs and shaving cream. I don't know why, but every year on Halloween, kids in the South Bronx would throw eggs at people. Usually big kids would throw eggs at smaller kids, and if they were really mean they would spray them with shaving cream. Throughout junior high school I was able to avoid it. I would take the long way home, avoid busy streets, hide out in the candy store, or just pretend to be sick so I wouldn't have to go to school. But in high school my luck ran out.

One day while walking home from school I noticed three girls behind me. They were older than me. I started to walk a little faster. They started to walk a little faster too. Then I started to walk really fast. Then they started to walk really fast. I was a few blocks away from my building—my sanctuary. I told myself it's now or never. So I made a run for it. The key to running is never looking back, but of course I looked back and next thing I know one of the girls was in front of me. The bitch outflanked me. I had no choice but to make a left turn, which unfortunately for me, left me in a dead-end street. The three girls surrounded me and blocked my escape. At this point I was only one block away from my building but I was trapped—trapped the same way Bastian was trapped by those three bullies in the alley in *The NeverEnding Story*. Fortunately for me there weren't any garbage dumpsters around. I thought to myself, now what? I needed a plan. There was no way I was going home covered in eggs and shaving cream. Just then the girl on the left said:

"I got the first throw."

In situations like these, time either goes really fast or really slow. In this case it started slow and then jumped to super speed. The girl grabbed an egg from her jacket pocket, wound her arm back as though she was a Major League baseball player, and threw the egg. Miraculously, I caught the egg and it didn't break. Maybe it was a bad egg, or maybe I just got lucky. After I caught the egg I immediately threw it back at the girl—POW, right in the kisser, as Ralph Kramden would say. Then with my notebook in my hand I made a run for it. The girl I hit was dazed and confused. The girl in the middle was the smallest, so I ran straight toward her with all my might. I knocked her down. All that remained was the girl on the right. She was the biggest and the ugliest. She threw an egg at me, but I used my notebook as a shield. Then, like Roddy Piper I poked her in the eyes with my thumb. Then I kneed her where the sun don't shine. Now I was home free. As I was running I felt something hit the back of my head. It was an egg—ugh! It came from the girl I nailed with the egg. I guess she wanted payback. You ever try washing egg out of your hair? Well, let me tell you it's no fun. Eh, I guess it could have been worse.

Religion

When I was fourteen years old, I had a talk with my mother about religion. I had just finished rereading the Bible, and there were several things I didn't agree with, so I asked my mother about them.

"Mom…"

"Jes, mija."

"Can I ask you some questions about the Bible?"

"Of course, mija."

"What does this passage mean? 'Your desire will be for your husband, and he will rule over you.' Genesis, chapter three, verse sixteen."

"It means you should only love your husband, and that you should be faithful to your husband."

"Doesn't that seem…sexist to you?"

"What do ju mean?"

"He will rule over you, what kind of shit is that?"

"Watch jur mouth!"

"I'm just saying, Mom. How come it doesn't say, 'Your desire will be for your wife.' This makes it seem like only the woman has to be faithful, and what about this passage: 'Wives submit to your husbands as to the Lord. For the husband is the head of the wife as Christ is the head of the church.' Ephesians, verses twenty-two and twenty-three."

"That one is more complicated."

"There's nothing complicated about it. It's religious submissive propaganda. It's basically comparing a man to God."

"Ay, Michelle, I think ju watch too much TV."

"It has nothing to do with watching television, and I have another question."

"What now?"

"Why does God have to be a man?"

"Because that's what it says in the Bible, that God is a man."

"Why can't God be a woman? I mean women are the ones that give birth. Yeah, I know, when it comes to sex it takes two, but once the guy drops off his sperm, he just takes off. After that the woman has to carry a fetus for nine months. We do all the heavy lifting. Or why can't there be two gods, a female god and a male god? At least that would be politically correct, and I have serious doubts about the Virgin Mary."

"Don't ju dare say anything bad about the Virgin Mary—don't ju you dare! She gave birth to our Lord and Savior, Jesus Christ."

"Mom, do you really think God swooped down to earth, impregnated some fourteen-year-old girl, and then happily floated back to heaven?"

"Don't be silly, Michelle. God didn't have...sex with the Virgin Mary."

"Oh, OK, so God impregnated the Virgin Mary without laying a finger on her?"

"Jes, it was a miracle."

"Let me ask you this, Mom, when the Virgin Mary got knocked up by God, she was married at the time, right?"

"Jes."

"So isn't that adultery and isn't adultery a sin?"

"Ay, Michelle, I don't want to talk to ju about this anymore. We are Catholics and those are the words of God."

Then my mother stormed out. After that we didn't talk about religion for a while. I think if I had been alive during medieval times, I would have been deemed a witch or some shit and I would have been burned alive.

Graffiti

In 1992, graffiti wasn't as prevalent as the 1970s or 1980s, but it was still around. That's when I started doing graffiti. It all started in science class. I was sitting in class—bored as usual, so I began doodling my name. As I was doodling a guy that was seated next to me saw what I was doing. He leaned over to me.

"Hey, do you write?"

"Huh?"

"Do you write?"

"Write what?"

"You know, graffiti."

"No, why would I write graffiti?"

"You're writing on that paper."

"Oh this? This is nothing, I'm just bored."

"It kinda looks like graffiti."

"Really?"

"Well, bad graffiti."

"Gee, thanks."

"You ever thought about writing graffiti?"

"No."

Then Mrs. González, our teacher, intervened.

"Ms. Perez, do you have something to say?"

"Uh, no, ma'am."

After Mrs. González resumed teaching, the boy leaned over to me again and said:

"We'll talk after class."

So we did. He introduced himself to me.

"My name is Jason."

"I'm Michelle."

"So you never thought about doing graffiti?"

"Nope, never."

"Let me ask you this, how would you like to be famous?"

"Famous, how?"

"So my real name is Jason, but my tag name is Jay 167."

"How did you come up with that name?"

"People call me Jay, it's my nickname, and I live on East 167th Street."

"Clever. So how will writing graffiti make me famous?"

"You come up with a tag name and you write your tag name everywhere, on trains, buses, walls, rooftops, in high up places where no one can reach, that's how you become famous."

"Sounds tempting. But what if I get caught?"

"If you get caught you do community service for a day or two. The trick is not to get caught."

"Have you ever gotten caught?"

"Nope. Never have, never will. So you interested?"

"Yeah, I'm interested."

"Meet me after school in the yard. We'll start with the basics."

So after school I meet with Jason and he began teaching me about graffiti. He called it graffiti 101. First I learned graffiti lingo: A "tag" is when someone writes their name on a surface, as in tagging or bombing. A "throw up" (not to be confused with vomiting) is much larger than a tag. A throw up is usually in the style of bubbled letters. A "piece" can be the same size as a throw up or it can be bigger, it all depends. But a piece has more colors and is more stylish than a throw up, basically it's more elaborate. Jason said a piece is a work of art. A "top to bottom" is when an entire train car is covered from top to bottom. Some people call a top to bottom a "blockbuster." A "burner" is also like a piece.

Burners are typically done on trains from the base of the train to the bottom of the window. And finally, there's a mural. A mural is a collection of pieces done by different graffiti artists, but a mural can also be done by just one artist. Sometimes a mural can have a theme. Murals are also done in remembrance of someone that passed away. Then there's the graffiti supplies, like fat caps and skinny caps. You would use a fat cap to fill in a throw up; it spreads the paint faster, and when you're writing on the wall illegally time is of the essence. Once you're done filling in the throw up, you would outline it with a skinny or regular cap. Of course fat caps could be used on pieces or burners also. Then there's black books. Black books were sketch books that graffiti artists used to draw in. So once I was up to par with all the graffiti lingo, I had to come up with a tag name for myself. One thing I liked about graffiti is that hardly any girls were doing it. So when people saw my name, I wanted them to know I was a girl. But I didn't want a girly name. Jason said I should use Lola, but Lola sounded like a porn star's name. Then I thought about Jason's name, Jay 162. Then it dawned on me, Niña 152. Why Niña 152? Well, because I'm a Spanish girl and I live on East 152nd Street. Jason liked it. Before I hit the streets I began to practice writing my name. Jason wanted me to study tags, throw ups, and pieces. We went all over the city. Almost every handball court in the Bronx had graffiti on it. The South Bronx High School had an entire wall filled with graffiti. In the Bronx graffiti writers like Cope, Bio, Wane, Ces, and Sento had their work everywhere. I really liked Sento's pieces. After my research was done Jason took me to this graffiti store in SoHo off Canal Street, and I bought my first black book and some fat caps. Before I started spray-painting and doing throw ups, I needed to get used to writing with a pilot marker. Unlike me, Jason stole all his supplies. Me, I wasn't that bold yet. So Jason gave me some of his markers and one night we just started tagging. The first thing I tagged was a billboard in the East 149th Street train station. I remember the first time I saw my name on the wall. I felt like a superstar. While I wrote, Jason looked out for the police, and I did the same for him. Within a month I was tagging with spray paint. Within two months I was doing throw ups. I was the Lady Pink of 1992—well, at least I was trying to be.

So every Friday and Saturday I would sneak out of my house at 2 a.m. and go bombing with Jason. Jason's dream was to bomb a train, but the era of bombing trains was gone. Train yards had fences and barbed wire. And even if you did manage to get into a train yard, the MTA would never let the train run with graffiti on it. However, once in a blue moon a graffiti writer managed to bomb a train, and that train would run.

One day me and Jason went all city. All city means bombing all five boroughs, but we didn't bomb Staten Island. To get to Staten Island you had to take the ferry, and there's only one train on Staten Island. Who the hell builds a borough with only one train? Anyway, we never hit Staten Island.

Within a year, I did my first piece. Jason took me to a secluded place, that way I could take my time. It was right behind South Bronx High School. There was a track there for freight trains, but the train rarely came. It was my first time on train tracks. Jason warned me about the third rail. He said, "Don't ever touch the third rail." Apparently one of his graffiti friends died when he accidently fell on the third rail. Anyway, so we jumped onto the track, walked about two hundred feet, and stopped at a wall. It was the perfect place to do a piece. No one could see us. It took me about an hour to complete the piece, and of course it sucked, but it didn't matter, it was my first piece. Jason said not to worry, your first piece always sucks unless you're a prodigy.

The highlight of my graffiti career was when me and Jason bombed a train yard. It was the 4 train at Bedford Avenue. The yard was surrounded by fences and had barbed wire on the top, so climbing over the fences was out. So what did Jason do? He brought a huge bolt cutter with him. I was impressed. So we staked out the train yard for an hour to make sure no cops or MTA workers were around. It was 4 a.m. on a Saturday. After we

51

made sure that no one was around we made our way to the fence. Jason cut the fence with the bolt cutter. After he cut the fence he pulled back the fence a little so I could get in, then he followed. Once we were inside the train yard I was in awe of all the trains; they looked massive. I felt so small. Once my awe dissipated, Jason and I went to work on the trains. First, we tagged some trains, then we did some throw ups, and last, we did our pieces. This was my fifth piece. I had gotten pretty good at doing pieces. Of course Jason was much better. After I was done with my piece I was about to take a picture of it, but then I heard something. I whispered to Jason.

"Did you hear that?"

"Yeah."

"What do you think it was?"

"I'm not sure."

I wanted to take a picture of my piece in case the train didn't run; the picture would be my only proof. I asked Jason:

"Should I take the picture?"

"If someone is there, they'll see the camera flash and spot us. Can you turn off the flash?"

"It won't come out good without the flash, it's too dark. I need this picture."

"Then go for it but be ready to run just in case."

So I stepped back as far as I could and I took the picture. Sure enough someone was there. They yelled:

"Hey, you!"

Me and Jason saw someone with a flashlight coming at us. We didn't stop to see who it was, we just ran like hell. As we reached the outside of the yard, we saw the number 4 train pulling into the train station. We ran to the station. Once we arrived at the station we jumped over the turnstile, ran up the stairs, and just as the train doors were closing we made it inside the train, and immediately the train started moving. It turns out the person chasing us was a cop; he was closer than we thought. If the train hadn't been in the station, he would have definitely caught us. As the train pulled off, Jason gave him the finger, just like when the Warriors outran the Turnbull ACs in the movie, *The Warriors*. We never knew if the trains we bombed ever left the yard but it didn't matter; we bombed a shitload of trains and I had the proof in my camera. While me and Jason made our way home I asked him:

"Hey Jay, can I ask you a question?"

"Sure."

"Why do you do graffiti, is it just to be famous or is it the thrill?"

"Look at where we live, Michelle. We live in the fucking ghetto. We don't have any opportunities, but I'd rather be doing graffiti than selling drugs, or beating people up in some bullshit gang. Also, graffiti is a way for me to express myself. Shit, maybe one day I'll be famous and they'll have my work in the MoMA or some other fancy museum. Maybe I'll even be able to make an honest living."

A week later Jason died. He was doing a piece on a bridge on Randall's Island. After he finished his piece he lost his footing and fell over five hundred feet. After that I stopping doing graffiti. Without Jason it just wasn't the same. But I have to be honest, every now and then I have the urge to go all city.

Puerto Rican History

The year was 1992. I was fifteen years old. It was a week before the Puerto Rican Day Parade. I had never been to the parade, but I'd heard good things about it, so I asked my mother if she was going to the parade.

"Mom, are you going to the parade?"

"The Puerto Rican Day Parade?"

"Yes."

"Ay no."

"What do you mean 'Ay no'?"

"Why should I go?"

"I dunno, to show everyone that you're proud to be Puerto Rican."

"I don't need to go to some silly parade to do that."

"What do you have against the parade?"

"Ju know, every year millions of people go to the Puerto Day Parade, meanwhile most of those people don't know anything about Puerto Rico."

"Yeah, but I'm sure that's not the case for everyone that goes to the parade."

"It is for most."

"But that shouldn't stop you from going—it's fun."

"What's fun about being surrounded by a million Puerto Ricans on a hot summer day?"

After my mother left I began to think about what she said. Maybe she was right. Maybe I should learn more about my heritage. So the following day I spoke to Ms. Cruz, my history teacher. Ms. Cruz taught American History, but she was also Puerto Rican, plus she's very sexy, so any excuse to talk to her was a good one.

"Ms. Cruz."

"Yes, Michelle."

"Do you know anything about Puerto Rican history?"

"As a matter of fact, I do. What would you like to know?"

"Well…everything."

"Oh OK. This may take a while, do you have some time?"

"For you, I have all the time in the world."

So me and Ms. Cruz talked for about two hours. Turns out Christopher Columbus discovered Puerto Rico in 1493, although some people prefer the term "invaded," kinda like when Christopher Columbus invaded the current United States and called the Native Americans "Indians" because he thought he was in India. Anyway, back to Puerto Rico. In 1493, a group of indigenous people called the Taínos lived in Puerto Rico. In 1508,

Spain began to colonize Puerto Rico. Spain enslaved the Taínos. Spain used the Taínos to mine for gold and do all their dirty work. They killed men, women, and children. Basically, what the Pilgrims and their ancestors did to Native Americans, Spain did to the Taínos. Fast forward to the Spanish-American War in 1898. During the Spanish-American War the U.S. invaded Puerto Rico. As a result, the U.S. gained Puerto Rico as a territory. Of course, the U.S. treated Puerto Rico like shit—ergo the Ponce Massacre of 1937. In 1952, the U.S. made Puerto Rico a commonwealth. What's a commonwealth? Well, it means Puerto Rico is a territorial possession; it's not a U.S. state. "Territorial possession," I don't like the way that sounds. Anyway, after our conversation I thanked Ms. Cruz for her time and I went home. Now of course there's more to Puerto Rican history than that; Ms. Cruz just gave me a glimpse. The following day Ms. Cruz gave me a book to read about Puerto Rican history.

The day of the parade I decided not to go. I watched the parade on TV with my mother; she liked the floats. After the parade was over I went to my room and began reading the book Ms. Cruz gave me.

Sex, Part One

When I was sixteen years old, I went to a gay bar on Christopher Street called the Stonewall Inn. My friend Justin told me about it. So after I got my fake ID, I took the E train to West 4th Street and walked to Christopher Street. I had never been to a bar, let alone a gay bar. I expected to see a bunch of half-naked men and women dancing in cages, with loud music playing, and people doing hard drugs while drinking alcohol. When I opened the door and walked in it was quite the opposite. I mean there was music playing and a small handful of people dancing, but it was very relaxed. After I got my bearings I made my way to the bar.

"Hi, can I have a beer?"

The bartender looked at me for a minute.

"How old are you?

"Twenty-one."

"Let me see your ID."

"Sure."

I took out my fake ID and handed it to the bartender. He looked at my ID and then he looked at me. Then he looked at my ID again.

"Happy birthday."

"Huh?"

"Today's your birthday, right?"

"Oh yeah, the big twenty-one."

"Happy birthday."

"Thank you."

"You came by yourself?"

"Yeah, but my friends are meeting me here later. They're taking me out for my birthday."

"Well, the first round is on the house."

"Thanks."

So the bartender handed me a beer. I looked at the beer for a moment, then I took a sip, then I almost spit it out. It tasted like piss—not that I know what piss tastes like. Just then a very beautiful woman sat next to me and handed me a drink.

"Try this."

"What is it?"

"It's called a Malibu Orange, it's a fruity drink."

I took a sip.

"Wow, that tastes great, thanks."

"You're welcome. By the way, I'm Esperanza."

Esperanza, there was something about that name I just found so…sexy.

"Doesn't Esperanza mean hope?"

"Yes, it does."

"I'm Michelle."

"Nice to meet you, Michelle. So, what brings you to the most famous gay bar in the United States?"

"This place is famous?"

"Sure is, don't you know anything about gay history?"

"Apparently not. So what's so special about this place?"

"There was a big riot here in the sixties."

"Really?"

"Yup. So you're here by yourself?"

"Yeah. One of my friends from high school—I mean college—told me about this place."

"It's OK. I got here the same way you did, with a fake ID."

"You're not twenty-one?"

"No, I'm nineteen. How old are you?"

"Well…I'm sixteen."

"Sixteen?"

"Yup."

"You look older."

"Thanks."

Me and Esperanza talked for about an hour. Turns out she was an aspiring artist. After we left the Stonewall Inn we went back to her place.

"Nice place."

"Thanks."

"You live here by yourself?"

"No, I have a roommate."

"Is she here?"

"No, she's at work. She won't be home until later tonight."

"Oh."

"My room is this way."

I followed Esperanza to her room. Her room was filled with paintings.

"Are all these paintings yours?"

"Yup."

"You're really talented."

"Thanks."

"What's your inspiration?"

"Well, I just paint whatever pops into my head."

"That's so cool. I wish I was that creative."

"You can be. Michelle, can I ask you a question?"

"Sure."

"Have you ever been with a woman?"

"Ummm, no."

"Have you ever been with a man?"

"No."

"But you're gay, right?"

"Yes, I just haven't come out yet. Well, my friend from high school knows, but that's it."

"Do you find me attractive?"

"Uh, yeah."

Then Esperanza kissed me. First, she kissed my bottom lip, then she kissed my top lip, lastly, she kissed both of my lips. Then she slowly unbuttoned my shirt. She kissed my collarbone, and then she worked her way up to my neck. Then she bit my ear softly. She took off my shirt and then my bra. Then she took my hand and led me to her bed. Once we were on her bed I expected to have sex right away, but instead she just caressed my body. It was very sensual. She unbuckled my belt, unzipped my jeans, and stuck her hand down my pants. It felt amazing. This was the moment I'd been waiting for ever since I realized I was gay, ever since that girl in junior high touched my hand. Then we had sex. Esperanza did most of the work. After we were done I gave Esperanza my number, but of course she never called. It didn't matter; I got to have sex with a woman. Best. Day. Ever.

Gay History

A few days after I lost my virginity, I started to think about what Esperanza said about gay history. She was right; I didn't know anything about gay history, so I decided to learn. Since Esperanza said there was a big riot at the Stonewall Inn in the sixties, I decided to start there. I went back to the Stonewall Inn. When I got to the Stonewall Inn the same bartender was there. I walked over to him.

"You're back."

"Yup."

"So how was your birthday?"

"It was great."

"Glad to hear it. So what brings you by?"

"So I heard there was a big riot here in the sixties, do you know anything about it?"

"Of course I do, I was here."

"Really?"

"Yup."

"How old were you?"

"I was sixteen."

"Sixteen? How did you get in?"

"Well, I looked older than sixteen, plus I had a fake ID."

"A fake ID?"

"Yeah, you know, like that one you showed me the last time you were here."

I smiled and remained quiet.

"Embarrassed?"

"Yup."

"Good."

"So...what happened here that night?"

"It was June 28, 1969. Back then you couldn't be gay in public, it was illegal."

"Illegal?"

59

"Yes, they called it 'lewd and immoral conduct.'"

"Who called it that?"

"Straight people."

"So you couldn't hold hands or kiss in public?"

"Nope. You could also get fired from your job for being gay, and if you were in the military, and they found out you were gay, you would get dishonorably discharged."

"Wow, I had no idea things were that bad."

"Gay people had no rights. So places like the Stonewall Inn were our sanctuary, even though gay bars were technically illegal."

"So how did the riot happen?"

"That night the police raided the Stonewall Inn. It wasn't the first time the Stonewall Inn was raided, but that night something different happened."

"What happened?"

"People fought back. The police arrested several people for lewd and immoral conduct. As they were walking them to the paddy wagon they were overrun by an angry crowd that was outside the Stonewall. Fearful for their lives, the police decided to go back into the Stonewall. They barricaded the door from the inside until help could arrive. The crowd outside the Stonewall grew bigger and bigger. At one point there were thousands of people outside. Many of them were trying to get in."

"Why were they trying get in?"

"They wanted to hurt the police. They were mad as hell and they weren't going to take it anymore. *Network*, 1976—great movie."

"Did they get in?"

"No, eventually a shitload of cops came in riot gear and the police officers inside were able to get out. But even after the police inside got out, it took a while for the police to disperse the crowd. People were throwing things at the police, starting fires, and destroying property."

"Then what happened?"

"Eventually the rioting stopped but the following day the riot continued. The following year we had the very first gay pride walk, it was June 28, 1970."

"Wow, that's amazing."

"I'm very proud to be a part of it. So now you know a little bit about gay history."

"Yeah, thanks for sharing."

"You're very welcome."

"Hey, since I'm here, how about a drink?"

"Sorry, kid, maybe in a couple of years."

Sex, Part Two

Earlier that year I had had sex with a woman—best thing that had ever happened to me, but I still hadn't come out to my family, especially my mother. I mean, how do you tell your religiously fanatical mother—who doesn't think the Bible is sexist, and who was born and raised in a small conservative town in Puerto Rico, and who married her first love at age twenty-two—that her only daughter is gay? I tried to imagine the best and worst-case scenarios. The best-case scenario would be if my mother said, "Oh Michelle, I'm so happy for ju. I always wanted a gay daughter." The worst-case scenario would be my mother killing me. The point being, if I'm gonna tell my mother that I'm gay, I have to be sure. But how do I know if I'm sure? I mean, I'm attracted to women. I've been with a woman but I've never been with a man. That's it! I'll sleep with a man. I'll see what all the hubbub is about. But who do I sleep with? I can't sleep with anyone from school—kids talk. And I can't sleep with anyone in the neighborhood. I'll have to go outside my school and outside my neighborhood. I got it! I'll go to Brooklyn. I know what you're thinking, Brooklyn is still in New York City, but have you ever traveled from the Bronx to Brooklyn? It's like a whole other country. Once I went to Coney Island with my friends—two hours on the train. Another time I went to Rockaway Beach—three hours! After that I was like, I'm never going to Brooklyn again. Anyway, the goal is to sleep with someone that isn't local, so I decided to go to Brooklyn. My cousin used to live in Brooklyn, so I asked her to recommend a club.

Now if I'm gonna have sex with a man, I would like the sex to be good. My cousin Rachel said it's all about the penis. But how do I choose the right penis? Most women agree that bigger is better, but I don't want some huge penis tearing up my vagina and ripping through my stomach like that creature in the movie *Alien*, with Sigourney Weaver. I want an average penis. But what's average? So I conducted a survey and here are the results: five inches or less is considered small. Six inches is considered average. Seven or eight inches is considered big. Eight or nine inches is considered very big. And anything bigger than nine inches is considered ginormous. And then there's the width, basically the wider the better. God, this is complicated. I didn't realize straight women placed so much emphasis on a man's penis. Not that men are any better, men love tits and asses, the bigger the better.

So how does one choose the perfect penis? Well I just decided to go with six inches. But how do I determine the size of a man's penis without seeing it. I mean, I can't just ask a guy, "Hey, how big is your penis?" Of course he'll lie. They say a man always adds two to three inches to his penis. So if a guy says his penis is seven inches it's really five inches. So I'll have to use the penis theory. The penis theory allows you to safely determine the size of a man's penis before seeing it. There are two penis theories. The first one has to do with a man's feet. Basically, the bigger his feet, the bigger his penis. Which is why some women like a guy with big feet. Then there's the hand theory. You measure the size of a man's hand from the base of his palm to tip of his middle finger. Which is why some women like a guy with big hands.

So I hit the club in Brooklyn. I looked older than sixteen, so of course I didn't have any trouble getting in. I wore a somewhat tight red dress with black heels. Of course a shitload of guys tried to pick me up or buy me drinks, but if I was going to have sex with a guy, I would prefer that it be a nice guy, or as nice as can be for a guy. I decided to do some reconnaissance by the bar. As I sat by the bar drinking my Malibu Orange, I noticed a guy on the other side of the bar. He was about five feet eight, olive skin, medium build, with short hair. There was nothing compelling about him. He was just an average-looking guy. He was drinking by himself. I watched him for about ten minutes. Not once did he ask a girl to dance—maybe he was gay? I decided to talk to him.

"Hi."

"Hi."

"I'm Michelle."

"David."

"So, David, come here often?"

"Actually, this is my first time. How about you?"

"It's my first time also. So what are you drinking?"

"Malibu Orange."

"No shit, me too."

"Really?"

"Yeah."

"Umm, so would you like to dance?"

"Sure."

So as we walked to the dance floor, "Oye cómo va" by Tito Puente began playing. David was a decent dancer. My mother always said a man should know how to dance. After we danced, we went back to the bar and talked. He didn't seem like other guys. He was quiet and reserved. So either he's the nicest guy in the world, or he is a serial killer. Either way, I came here to have sex with a man to reinforce my homosexuality.

"David, can I ask you a question?"

"Sure."

"What size is your dick?"

"What?"

Rather than play that stupid guessing game I decided to use a more straightforward approach. You should have seen his face.

"Your dick, what size is it, how many inches?"

"Uh, why do you want to know?"

"Because I'm considering having sex with you, but I need to know how big your dick is first."

"Oh OK. Well…um, I would say it's seven inches."

"Seven inches?"

"Or eight—maybe eight."

"Great!"

That meant it was six inches. The perfect size for my ideal penis.

"Can we go back your place?"

"My place?"

"Yes."

"Do you live alone?"

"Well, actually I live with my parents, but they're on vacation in Spain."

"So your place it is."

Poor David, he looked dumbfounded, but I was on a mission to have sex. Later that night we arrived at David's apartment. I followed him to his room, he turned on the lights, and I was blown away. On his wall were movie posters of *Godzilla*, *Star Wars*, and *Jaws*. On his shelf were VHS tapes of *Back to the Future (Parts 1, 2, and 3)*, *Weird Science*, and *Star Trek II: The Wrath of Khan*. My favorite part from *Star Trek II* was when Captain Kirk yells "Khaaaaan!" He also had quite the comic-book collection. He had X-Men, Iron Man, and The Incredible Hulk comics. He had X-Men 101, the first appearance of Jean Grey as the Phoenix. He even had The Incredible Hulk 181 (the first appearance of Wolverine). I was impressed. David was a freshman at New York University. He wanted to be a film

64

director. He was eighteen years old. After I finished admiring his comic-book collection, I asked him:

"Do you have any condoms?"

David reached under his bed, grabbed an Adidas sneaker box, and opened it. It was filled with condoms.

"Is this enough?"

"Uh, yeah, I think that's enough."

I set the box down and then I kissed him softly. First, I kissed his bottom lip, then I kissed his top lip, then I kissed both his lips. Even though this was just a sexual experiment to confirm my homosexuality, I wanted to make the best of it. David kissed my shoulder and slowly made his way to my neck. Not bad, I thought to myself. After we kissed for a few minutes we undressed each other. Then we sat down on his bed. We kissed for few more minutes. Of course he copped a feel of my breast, but at least he didn't squeeze it with brute force; he was gentle. Then I lay down on David's bed. I took off my underwear. David took off his Calvin Klein Marty McFly underwear and then he grabbed a condom, put it on, and went in for the kill. So I just waited, and waited, and waited.

"Is everything OK?"

"Well…"

"Well what?"

"I can't find the hole."

"By hole, do you mean my vagina?"

"Uh…yeah."

"Have you done this before?"

"Umm…no."

"Did you say no?

"Yes."

"So you're a virgin?"

"Well…yeah."

"Do you want me to stick it in for you?"

"No, no, no, I can find it—just give me a minute…or two."

David tried again.

"Ouch!"

"What?!"

"That's the wrong hole!"

"The wrong hole?! You mean there's more than one?!"

David started to panic. My sexual experiment was on the verge of collapsing. So I grabbed his penis and placed it inside my vagina. Happily, he moaned.

"Whoa."

"You OK?"

"Yeah, I'm good."

"How's it feel?"

"…Warm."

"So are you ready?"

"Ready."

David was very tense. You could tell he was trying to remember what he had learned from all those years of watching porn. In and out. In and out. Five minutes later he came. We ended up having sex six times that night. Thankfully David lasted longer each time. I think his longest was thirty minutes. Was it good? Eh, it was OK. I guess the actual act was good, but I wasn't attracted to David. Not because he was ugly or anything like that, but because he was a man. After we were done I got dressed.

"You're not staying over?"

"Nah, I gotta head home—curfew and all."

"Oh, I understand. So when will I see you again?"

"Umm, I dunno."

"Well, can I have your phone number?"

David took out his little black book and handed it to me. I saw the look on his face. He was like a sad puppy desperately seeking attention from his owner. He wanted me to be his girlfriend, or at the very least he wanted to have sex again sometime in the very near future. I wrote down a fake number and handed the book back to him.

"Here you go."

66

"Thanks."

"Hey. If you wanna catch a movie or grab a bite, I'm free Monday after my screenwriting class."

"Uh, I'm busy on Monday, sorry."

"Oh OK. Maybe another time then."

That's when I realized it. That's when I realized the power of the vagina. Once a man gets a taste of it, there's no going back. They can't live without it. They have to have it every waking second of their lives. And if they don't get it—forget about it, they turn into Mr. Hyde. Wars have been started for less. Still, I felt bad for David; he was a nice guy, but the whole point of this sexual experiment was to validate my homosexuality, and that was exactly what it did. Now I just have to tell my mother that I'm gay. Yeah, I'm looking forward to that.

Coming Out, Part One

Today is the day. Today is the day I tell my mother that I'm gay. Well, here goes nothing.

"Mom, can I talk to you for a minute?"

"Of course, mija."

"Maybe you better sit down."

"Is everything OK?"

"Well, that depends on your point of view."

"Mija, ju can tell me anything."

"You sure about that, Mom?"

"Jes, of course."

"OK, well here goes. Mom…I'm gay."

"Gay, what do ju mean gay?"

"You know, gay."

"Doesn't gay mean happy?"

"It means I like women, Mom."

"Ju like women?"

"Yes."

"So ju like women instead of men?"

"Yes."

"No, no, no, no. Ju are not gay!"

"Yes, I am."

"No, ju are not! Two women can't be together."

"Why not?"

"Because two women can't make a baby. Ju need a man and woman."

"No, you don't."

"Jes, ju do. Ju need the, the, the thing from the man."

"Sperm?"

"Jes. Ju need lots of sperm."

"Well, technically you only need one sperm cell, but that's beside the point. Nowadays there's in-vitro fertilization and there's adoption."

"In-vitro que?"

"In-vitro fertilization. It's when they take a man's sperm and place it in—"

"Ay, enough with the sperm talk! You can't be gay because being gay is a sin. It says so in the Bible. 'A man cannot have sex with another man. It's an abomination.' Leviticus, chapter 20 verse 13."

"Yeah, but it doesn't say anything about a woman having sex with another woman."

"Have ju had sex with a woman?"

"No, of course not, Mother."

As you already know, that was a total lie.

"Then how would ju know if ju like women?"

"I just know."

"Ah! Ju know nothing!"

And then my mother stormed out.

"So you're not throwing me out?"

After that my mother didn't talk to me for two months.

Coming Out, Part Two

So I told my mother that I'm gay, now all I have to do is tell my father. My father wasn't as religiously conservative as my mother, so I was hoping it would go better. I went to go see him at his apartment.

"Hey, Dad."

"Hey."

"So…whatcha doing?"

"Oh, just organizing my fishing hooks."

"Do you need help?"

"No, I'm OK."

"You sure you don't need help?"

"No."

"So…how's work?"

"Work is OK.

"Do you need money?"

"No, Dad, I don't need money."

"Because if you do it's OK."

"Dad, I don't need any money."

"Then why are you acting so strange?"

"Well, there's something I have to tell you."

"Something bad?"

"Well…"

"Are you pregnant? So help me God, Michelle, if you're pre—"

"No, Dad, I'm not pregnant."

"Are you a drug addict?"

"Dad, do I look like a drug addict?"

"Then what is it?"

"Dad…I'm…gay."

"You're gay?"

"Yes."

"As in 'you like women' gay?"

"Yes."

"So you're a dyke?"

"Dad, the word 'dyke' is a derogatory word."

"You're a dyke. I should have known. You were always such a tomboy. I just figured you'd grow out of it. I should have never let you play with boy toys, and I should have never taught you how to fight when you were in elementary school."

"Dad, I'm not a dyke!"

"So you're one of those feminine lesbians, the ones that go out with dykes?"

"Dad, stop trying to put me into some type of...category."

"How do you know you're gay? You've never even been with a boy."

I remained silent. My father saw the look on my face.

"You have been with a boy! Who is he?! Where is he?! I'll kill him!"

"Dad, it's no one you know and besides he's actually a nice guy. You probably would have liked him."

"What makes you think I would like any boy that sleeps with my daughter, and what are you doing have sex anyway? You're only sixteen."

"So, you had sex when you were fifteen."

"I did not."

"Yes, you did, Tio Poncho told me two years ago at the Christmas party. Tio Poncho had a lot of coquito that night."

"That son of a bitch."

"Tio Poncho said she was the ugliest girl in Ponce."

"Enough about me, we're talking about you. So you had sex with a boy and you didn't like it. That doesn't mean you're gay. Don't you need something to compare it to, like having sex with a girl?"

I remained quiet again.

"Ay, Michelle, what are you trying to do to me? Did you have sex with both of them on the same day?"

"No, not on the same day."

70

"And here I thought you were this innocent little—"

"Virgin?"

"I was gonna say princess but virgin works too."

"Dad, I've known I was gay since junior high school. Does being gay make me a bad person?"

"No."

"Now that you know I'm gay, will you stop loving me?"

"No, of course not."

"Then what's the problem?"

"It's just that I always imagined giving you away at your wedding, being there when you had your first child, and teaching your kids how to fish and build toy models—the good ones, not those cheap two-dollar models."

"You can still give me away at my wedding, it'll just be to a woman—assuming they ever make gay marriage legal in New York City. And as for my kids you can still teach them how to fish and build toy models."

"But how can two women have kids?"

"Here we go again."

Long story short, my father accepted me for being gay. It didn't happen overnight but it happened. As for my mother, we just never talked about it, at least not for a while. Maybe not talking about it was her way of denying it.

Valentine's Day

On February 14, 1993, six people in my building were murdered. They were killed execution-style, one bullet each to the back of the head. I was fifteen years old. Three of them were my friends: Gabriela, age seventeen; Daniel, age fifteen; and Samuel, age seventeen. It happened in Samuel's apartment. Samuel lived in the apartment directly across from me. His apartment was five feet away from my apartment.

It happened at 12:30 a.m. I was up late that night. I was always up late. I was watching TV. I don't remember what I was watching. I heard what sounded like gunfire. I thought it was someone firing blanks in the hallway or maybe fireworks. I thought to myself, no way that's gunfire, not in my building, not in my hallway, but it was. I left my bedroom and walked to the living room. I looked into the eyehole. I saw Samuel's apartment door. Everything seemed OK. I wanted to open the door to see if something was happening in the hallway, but my instinct told me not to, so I didn't. So I went back to my room and resumed watching TV.

The next day I left my house early in the morning. It was Valentine's Day, and I was going to spend time with my friends. When I returned home that evening, my mother was in the hallway crying. She ran to me and said, "Michelle, they killed Gabriela. They killed Gabriela!" The other three people that were killed were Samuel's mother, sister, and his sister's boyfriend. Daniel had been down in the lobby that night. Apparently, the gunman grabbed Daniel and used him to gain entry into Samuel's apartment. In the worst way, he was in the wrong place at the wrong time. I still couldn't believe this happened in my building. I knew I lived in a bad neighborhood, but this happened less than five feet away from me. I felt so…violated.

Prom

Prom: an American tradition, the last goodbye, the rite of passage, the beginning of adulthood. The question is, should I go to prom? What do people do at prom anyway? I'll tell ya what they do: they eat, drink, dance, and get laid. Why do I have to go to prom to do that? I can do that any time. The fact of the matter is, prom is for straight people. Still, I wanted to go to my prom. The problem was, no one in my high school (except for Justin) knew I was gay. Justin was the only openly gay person in high school. Things hadn't been easy for Justin. He had been bullied often because of his sexuality. I guess it didn't help that he was very flamboyant and sometimes dressed like a male Celia Cruz, but to each his own. Anyway, I had two options: the first was not to go to prom at all, and the second was to go with a guy, ugh! I didn't wanna go with a guy. That's so fucking lame. It was 1996, not 1956. People didn't get arrested for being gay (at least not in the United States). So one day after school I spoke to Justin about prom.

"Hey, Justin, you got a minute?"

"Sure, anything for you."

"Are you going to prom?"

"Nah."

"But it's our senior year."

"What's so special about prom anyway?"

"It's the last time we'll see our friends from high school."

"No, the last time we'll see our friends from high school is at graduation."

"Yeah, but it's not the same."

"Well, if it means that much to you, I'll go with you to prom."

I thought about Justin's offer for a moment.

"Thanks, but I wanna go to prom with another girl."

"Who you gonna go with?"

"I don't know. I don't know any gay girls at Graphics."

"There are plenty of lesbos at Graphics, they're just in the closet, like you."

"How do you know they're gay?"

"Gaydar."

"What's gaydar?"

"Girl, you have a lot to learn. I'll make a list of all the gay girls at Graphics, and I'll give it to you tomorrow."

"Thanks."

"Anytime, sugar."

The next day Justin gave me the list, and there were four girls on it. Now the question was, who do I ask to the prom? I mean, you just can't take anyone to the prom. Prom was in three months, so I had some time. I looked at the list; two of the girls were freshmen, so I crossed them out—no one wants to go to prom with a freshman. So that just left two girls. One of them was a senior by the name of Sofia. The other one was a sophomore by the name of Irene. My goal was to get to know them individually and see if there was any chemistry between us. I began with Irene. During lunch, I saw Irene eating by herself. I asked if I could join her and she said yes. Little by little we got to know each other. One day we were hanging out by the West Side Highway, just watching cars go by. By then we had already hung out a few times. I couldn't speak for Irene, but there was chemistry for me. But Irene was still in the closet. So while me and Irene were hanging out I decided to talk to her about it. I decided to try a somewhat direct approach.

"So when did you realize you were gay?"

"What?"

"When did you realize you were gay?"

"Gay? I'm not gay. What makes you think I'm gay?"

"Gaydar."

"Look, Michelle, I don't know what kind of game you're playing here but I'm not gay."

"Is there something wrong with being gay?"

"No, it's just that…I don't want people spreading rumors about me, and both of my parents are super religious."

"So are you or are you not gay?"

"Well, if I were, I wouldn't want anyone to know."

I looked at Irene for a moment. I was disappointed in her, but how can I be disappointed in her without being disappointed with myself? Except for my parents and Justin no one knew that I was gay. Then Irene asked me:

"You're not gonna tell everyone at school that I'm gay, right?"

74

"No."

"Swear?"

"Cross my heart and hope to die."

"Thank you."

"You're welcome. Instead I'm gonna tell everyone that I'm gay."

And that's exactly what I did. I told all my friends from Graphics that I was gay, and they told their friends, and their friends told their friends. Of course after that things changed. As I walked down the hallway everyone gave me a look; it kinda reminded me of that song "She's Got the Look" by Roxette. As I walked down the hallway, girls sucked their teeth, and guys drooled over me. Of course some guys offered to make me straight by having sex with them; suffice to say I refused their kind offers. I became the most famous person in school, for about a week—high-schoolers have a short attention span. As for prom, I had one month left to find a date, and I was determined now more than ever to go to prom with a girl. So, I set my eyes on Sofia. With Sofia, I tried a less direct approach. I didn't want to scare her off. One day during recess I saw Sofia playing handball in the handball court. She had just beaten one of the guys, which impressed me. I asked if I could play against her. Sofia looked at me for a moment. Although Sofia was a senior, we didn't have any classes together, so we didn't know each other, but I was sure she had heard that I was gay. After a moment, she said yes and we played handball until recess was over. Neither of us won the game; it was a tie. After that, we became friends. I liked her, and I got the impression that she liked me.

One day I invited Sofia to the movies to see *Scream*. There was a two-dollar movie theater two blocks away from our school. During the car scene (when Sidney was trapped in the Jeep and the killer came in through the back), Sofia jumped and grabbed my hand. She didn't let go. I took advantage of this opportunity. I began to caress her hand. I realize there's nothing romantic about

75

caressing hands during a horror movie, but it just felt like the right moment. Sofia looked at my hand and then she looked at me. Then out of nowhere she kissed me. Sofia had never kissed a girl before. After the movie, I spoke to Sofia about prom.

"Sofia."

"Yeah."

"Who are you going to prom with?"

"I dunno, Alfred from my English class asked me to go with him."

"What did you tell him?"

"I told him I would think about it."

"Why don't we go to prom together?"

"Won't everyone stare at us?"

"Probably, but I don't care. I know you haven't come out yet, but what better way to come out than at prom?"

"You're a bold one, Michelle Perez."

Sofia thought about it for a minute then she replied:

"OK. I'll go with you."

"Great!"

"What are we gonna wear?"

"Good question."

So today's the big day, prom day. Me and Sofia decided to keep it simple, no limo or stupid corsages. Just us and our simple fitted dresses. We also decided to meet at prom individually rather than go together. I arrived at the school at 6:00 p.m., and sure enough Sofia wasn't there. So I walked around, drank soda, and mingled with some friends. Thirty minutes later—still no Sofia. I was stood up. I guess Sofia didn't want to be embarrassed. Just then Sofia walked in. She looked beautiful. She walked toward me.

"Sorry I'm late."

"I thought you changed your mind."

"No, the cab was stuck in traffic."

"Oh OK. You look beautiful."

"You too."

"Thanks. So…do you wanna dance?"

"I thought you'd never ask."

Me and Sofia walked hand-in-hand onto the dance floor. While we were dancing, everyone stopped what they were doing and began to stare. Some people gave us dirty looks, but no one said anything. The looks didn't bother me or Sofia, we were in our own little world.

After prom was over, I used my fake ID to rent a room in a nice hotel. After some sensual kissing and caressing, me and Sofia had sex. It was her first time. Afterward we just lay in bed, cuddling. We didn't speak at all. Sofia was going to attend college in San Diego, California. She was leaving next week. I was very sad to see her go. Two months later I started college.

College Life

On August 31, 1996, I started college. College was very different from high school. You could come to class late (depending on the professor), and you could leave class early. You could smoke cigarettes on campus; not that I smoked cigarettes anyway— except for that one day when I was fourteen. There was so much freedom.

I was attending Lehman College in the Bronx. The campus was beautiful. My major was accounting. God, accounting is so boring. Like all parents, my mother wanted me to be a lawyer, or a doctor, but I didn't know what I wanted to do with my life. My mother said, "Ju have to study something, so ju can get a job and move out." Gee, thanks, Mom. So, I chose accounting.

Despite all the freedom, my first year at college was actually pretty boring. I missed Sofia and it took a while to make friends. Little did I know my life would drastically change.

Domestic Abuse

Fast-forward to 1997. I was nineteen years old, and I was a sophomore in college. One day while on the train I met a woman by the name of Angie. She was twenty-five years old. She had long black hair, luscious lips, and beautiful olive skin; turned out she was an accountant. So before I got off the train she asked me for my phone number, and a few days later we went on our first date. She was smart, sensitive, and funny. We hit it off right away. She always made me laugh. A year later she asked me to move in with her. Part of me felt that it was too soon, but by the same token, I was dying to get out of my mother's house. So I said yes.

After I moved in with Angie, things slowly began to change. First, she didn't want me working—even though I only had a part-time job at the time. Then she didn't want me wearing makeup. Now I hated makeup anyway, but I did wear lipstick. But Angie didn't even want me wearing lipstick. Then Angie didn't want me hanging out with my friends or speaking to them. The only person I was allowed to see was my mother. I asked myself, "What did I get myself into?" But I loved Angie, or at least I thought I did, so I wanted to make it work. Then finally the abuse started in. First it was verbal abuse. One day she came home from work angry, and she didn't like the food I'd cooked, so she smashed the plate on the floor, and began yelling and cursing at me. She didn't hit me, but I was afraid that she would. Not long after that, she started hitting me. It was strange; one minute she's laughing and smiling, the next she's hitting me. Certain things would just set her off. After she hit me, she always apologized for it. She said it'd never happen again. But that was always a lie. One day, while ironing her blouse, I accidently burned it. She took the iron and placed it on my arm. It was only for a second or two but felt like an eternity. After she burned my arm, she took me to the hospital. She told the nurse I accidently burned myself. I was tempted to tell the nurse what really happened, but Angie wouldn't let me speak, and I was scared of what she might do if I told the nurse the truth.

The breaking point was when I came home late one day from visiting my mother. My mother was home battling the flu, so I stayed with her a bit longer. When I got home, Angie was waiting outside the building. She asked me where I was and accused me of seeing another woman. After we entered the building, she started hitting me just outside our apartment door. Then she pushed me down the stairs. My left arm and the left side of my torso were in a lot of pain. A neighbor saw Angie push me down the stairs and called 911. An ambulance came and took me to the hospital. The police met me at the hospital. While I was waiting to be seen, a female police officer came to speak to me.

"Michelle Perez?"

"Yes."

"Hi, I'm Officer Hernandez."

"Hi."

"So what happened today?"

"I...I—"

Angie intervened:

"She fell—she fell down the stairs."

"How did you fall?"

Angie intervened again:

"She just tripped."

The police officer looked at Angie for a moment. She knew something wasn't right. She asked Angie:

"What's your relationship to Michelle?"

"I'm her girlfriend."

"I see. Can you wait outside?"

"Wait outside?"

"Yes."

"I'd rather not leave her alone right now."

"I'll be with her."

"With all due respect, I'd rather not wait outside."

"With all due respect, I'm telling you to wait outside."

79

Angie looked at the officer, and after a moment she left the room. It was just me and the police officer.

"So what really happened, Michelle?"

"I don't know what you're talking about."

"Michelle, I spoke to your neighbor. She said your girlfriend pushed you down the stairs."

"No, I tripped."

The police officer looked at me for a second, and then she asked me:

"Did you go to PS 161?"

"What?"

"Did you go to PS 161, on Tinton Avenue?"

"Yeah, why?"

"Did you live at 645 Prospect, apartment 615?"

"Yeah, how did you know?"

"I'm Jessica Hernandez."

"My bully?"

"Yup."

"Oh my God—wow, you lost so much weight. I didn't even recognize you."

"Yeah, I get that a lot. So...are you gonna tell me what really happened?"

"I'm...I'm not sure what you mean."

"Michelle, my father abused me for many, many years, then one day you show up at my doorstep and everything changed. You saved me, let me do the same for you."

Jessica convinced me to press charges against Angie. Angie was arrested. As for me I was discharged with a broken left arm and three bruised ribs on my left side. While Angie was in jail I used that opportunity to move out. My parents helped me move. All the furniture belonged to Angie, so I just took my clothes, books, and personal things. As for Angie, she was sent to prison for six months and was put on probation. People always ask me, "Why did you stay with her despite the abuse? Why didn't you just leave?" To be honest, I don't know. You never think you'll be in a situation like that, and then, when you are…well, things don't always go as planned.

Acting

After I left Angie, I moved back in with my mother. I was still attending school. I was depressed and believe it or not, I missed Angie. So one day while walking by the school theater, I saw a sign for auditions. It was the play *Real Women Have Curves*. It was for the role of Ana. At this point I was willing to try anything to get my mind off Angie, so I figured, what better way than to pretend to be someone else? Being that I never studied acting before in my entire life, I was positive that I wouldn't get the role, but I figured, what the hell. Come audition day I signed my name on the audition sheet, someone gave me a piece of paper with dialogue on it, or as actors called it, "sides," and I studied the side until I was called in to audition. I was very nervous. I introduced myself and then I began reading from the side with an actor. After the audition the director asked me some questions.

"Michelle, do you have any acting experience?"

"No."

"Have you ever studied acting?"

"No."

"What made you audition for this play?"

"Well, I guess I just wanted a change of pace, to try something new, does that makes sense?"

"Yes, it does."

"I still have some more people to audition, but I would just like to say that you have great presence."

"Thank you."

"If you get the part someone will notify you in a few days."

After the audition, I felt very good about myself. A few days later the director called me; I got the part.

Fast-forward to opening night. The music started to play, the lights came up, and the show began. It went very well. Both of my parents attended the show; of course they didn't sit together. After the show, I met my parents outside the theater. My mother hugged me.

"Mija, ju were wonderful. Ju were even better than Salma Hayek."

"Your mother is right, Michelle, you were wonderful."

"Thanks, you guys."

That's when I realized I wanted to do acting for the rest of my life. So I changed my major to theater. I graduated a year late but whatever—I was happy. I found my passion and I was pursuing it.

Rape

A year after the show I was entrenched in theater classes, but I loved every minute of it. I made many friends within the theater department. One of my good friends was Christina. Like me, Christina wanted to be an actor. One day while in acting class Christina reached over to me.

"Michelle, can I talk to you after class?"

Christina looked upset.

"Sure. Is everything OK?"

"We'll talk later."

After class, we found some steps outside the theater building and Christina told me what happened.

"So you know that I've been seeing Derrick, right?"

"Yeah."

"I mean we're not actually a couple, we just hang out every now and then."

"I get it. You guys aren't boyfriend and girlfriend but you have sex."

"Exactly. So, last week I was at Derrick's place and while we were having sex things got a little rough."

"A little rough?"

"Well, very rough."

"Did you ask him to stop?"

"Yes."

"Did he stop?"

"No."

"How many times did you ask him stop?"

"A few times?"

"Is it possible he didn't hear you?"

"I said it very loudly—he heard me. I said 'stop' and I said 'no,' but no matter what I said he wouldn't stop."

"Christina, that's rape. Did you tell the police?"

"No."

"Well, why not?"

"I don't know. After he was done I just left. I didn't know what to do."

"Come on."

"Where are we going?"

"To the police precinct, you're gonna press charges."

So I went with Christina to the police precinct, and after we told the officer at the front desk what happened, a detective came down to speak to Christina. He wasn't too sympathetic.

"So let me get this straight. You and this boy, Derrick, have been sleeping together for a few weeks, and last week you two had consensual sex, and now you want him arrested for rape?"

"Well...yeah."

I intervened.

"Why do you have to say it like that?"

"Like what?"

"Like you don't believe her."

"It's not that I don't believe her, it's just that they had consensual sex. They've been having consensual sex for weeks."

"So what, doesn't no mean no?"

"Yes, it does."

"And when someone tells you stop, shouldn't you stop?"

"Yes."

"Then what the fuck is the problem?"

"Look, we get a lot of false claims of rape—now I'm not saying this is a false claim, but what I am saying is, it may be difficult to prove that she was raped."

"What about a rape kit?"

"In order for a rape kit to be effective it has to be done within ninety-six hours, it's been a week."

"So now what?"

"Now I bring Derrick in for questioning."

Christina and I left the precinct. As I walked Christina home, she didn't seem very optimistic.

"This was a waste of time."

"Why would you say that, Christina?"

"You heard what the detective said. Derrick is probably gonna walk."

"You don't know that."

"Yeah, I do."

"Look, the detective said he'll call tomorrow, right?"

"Yeah."

"So let's just wait until tomorrow, OK?"

"OK, but I still think it was a waste of time."

Christina decided not to tell her parents that day. The following day the detective called Christina, and we went back to the precinct. Apparently Derrick claimed that he didn't hear Christina say "stop" or "no." The detective said Christina could get a lawyer, but it was very unlikely he'll be charged with anything. Later that night Christina told her parents what happened. Needless to say, her parents were devastated. Since the justice system failed Christina, her parents tried to get Derrick expelled from school, but since Derrick was never convicted of a crime, the school said their hands were tied. So Derrick walked, and Christina was right; it was all just a waste of time. So much for women's rights.

Payback

After Christina's rapist wasn't charged, I was pissed. I was angry and I needed to do something. Then a face popped into my mind, the face of Eddie Sanchez, the piece of shit who molested me in the church when I was ten years old. So that Sunday I went to the church again. It was 10:30 a.m., and mass was already underway. Everyone was sitting down, listening to Father Rodriguez give his sermon. It was a full house that day. I entered the church quietly, and I slowly walked to the front, checking each row on the left and right side, looking for Eddie. Finally, I found him. It would have been nice if I had superpowers like Storm from the X-Men; I would have electrocuted his ass with a bolt of lightning. But I didn't. Seated behind Eddie was my mother. Eddie looked at me for a few seconds and said:

"Michelle, is that you?"

I looked at Eddie for a moment, then I clenched my first, pulled my arm back, and then I punched him in the face with all my might. My mother yelled.

"Michelle! What are ju doing?!"

I ignored my mother. I punched Eddie in the face a second time, then a third time, shit, even a fourth time. Even Father Rodriguez yelled.

"What the hell is going on here?!"

I was going for a fifth punch, but someone grabbed me from behind and moved me away from Eddie. I was out of punching range but I wasn't out of kicking range, so I kicked Eddie in the groin. Eddie bent over in pain. I tried to kick Eddie again, but someone else grabbed my legs. My mother yelled at me again.

"Michelle, ju stop this right now!"

"He molested me!"

"What?"

"He molested me when I was ten years old!"

Of course Eddie protested.

"She's lying."

"Why would I lie?"

"So why did you wait until now to say something? I heard about you, you're a lesbian—you're a sinner. Are you gonna believe this sinner over me?"

Just then a girl a few years younger than me stood up and spoke.

"He molested me too."

Then a teenage girl stood up and spoke.

"Me too."

And finally, a young girl about ten years old stood up and spoke.

"He did the same thing to me last week."

Then my mother did something I never saw her do before in my entire life. She punched Eddie in the face, while yelling at him, "Hijo de puta!" She tried to punch him again but someone held her back. Eventually the police arrived, and I explained what happened. The police decided to arrest Eddie. As they were putting the handcuffs on Eddie, he told the police officer:

"I wanna press charges."

The police officer asked Eddie:

"You want to press charges, for what?"

"Those two women assaulted me."

The police officer asked a woman in the church.

"Ma'am, did you see anything?"

"No, I didn't see anything."

The police officer asked a man in the church.

"Sir, did you see anything?"

"I no see nothing."

Then the police officer asked Father Rodriguez.

"Father, did you see anything?"

Father Rodriguez looked at Eddie for a moment and then he said:

"No, officer, I didn't see anything. Please take him away."

As Eddie was being escorted out of the church by the police in handcuffs, myself and everyone in the church just watched. Later that day I arrived home with my mother.

"Michelle, why didn't ju tell me?"

"I don't know."

"What do ju mean, ju don't know?"

"I didn't want to talk about it?"

"First I learn that, that puta de madre Angie was abusing ju and now this. Is there anything else ju're not telling me?"

"I felt ashamed, OK! Is that what you wanna hear? I felt like it was my fault."

"Michelle, it wasn't jur fault. I just wish ju had said something sooner. Look at all those girls Eddie hurt after ju."

"Well, how come you and Dad never talked to me about child molestation or domestic abuse?"

"Are ju saying it's me and jur father's fault?"

"You know what, Mom, I can't do this right now, I just can't."

I began to walk out.

"Michelle where are ju going? Michelle! Michelle!"

I needed to get away from my mother. So I left the house, walked to the train station at East 149th Street and Prospect, and I took the uptown 6 train. After I got off at Pelham Bay, I walked toward City Island. I stopped at the drawbridge, and I stood there until the sun came down. I thought about what my mother said, and she was right. I should have said something sooner. When Eddie molested me as a child I wasn't prepared to deal with it; I guess no one is. All I can do now is try to move forward.

My Father

My father and I have a lot in common. We both like *The Honeymooners*. We both like a well-cooked pernil. And we both like women. The thing about my father is he likes women a little too much. When I was a young child I can remember my father flirting with women whenever my mother wasn't around. Of course back then I didn't know it was flirting. I just figured the women thought my father was very funny. Then as I got older he stopped flirting with women, at least when I was around. I was always curious as to why men cheat on their wives or girlfriends, so one day I talked to my father about it.

"Dad, can I ask you a question?"

"Sure."

"Why did you cheat on Mom?"

"Oh…that question."

"Well, it's hard to explain."

"Come on, Dad, I'm graduating from college in a few months, it's time you told me."

"Well, because I like women."

"I like women too but I've never cheated on any of my girlfriends."

"Yeah, but it's different for a woman."

"Dad, that's sexist."

"Why do you wanna know?"

"Dad, because of you we're not a family. I deserve to know."

"Fine. So even though I cheated on your mother—"

"Several times."

"Yes, several times.

"With different women."

"Yes. Even though I cheated on your mother several times with different women, I still loved her."

"But didn't you know cheating on her would hurt her?"

"I did."

"Then why would you want to hurt someone you love?"

"Michelle, love is complicated."

"Why is love complicated? If you loved Mom like you say you did, then you shouldn't have cheated on her."

"Life isn't black and white."

"Who's talking about life? I'm talking about love."

"Love, life, it's all the same shit."

"You're stalling, Dad. Why did you cheat on Mom?"

"I just got tired of...her."

"Her what?

"You know...her."

"You got tired of her what? Her cooking, her novelas, her singing Celia Cruz in the shower, what?"

"No, just...her."

"Ohhhh, you got tired of her vagina."

"Michelle!"

"You wanted fresh meat."

"I never said that."

"But that's what you meant."

"Michelle, sometimes when you're with a person for a long time you get...tired of the same thing. Sometimes you want something...different."

"I get it, Dad, but if you lacked the ability to be faithful why did you get married? Why not just stay single and date?

"Because I wanted a family. I wanted someone to be there when I came home from work."

"Hmph, I see. So how are things with your second wife?"

"Umm, well..."

"You're getting divorced, aren't you?

"Yeah."

"Let me guess, you cheated on her?"

"Yes, but only once."

"Once?"

"OK twice."

"Well, at least you're improving."

Yup, me and my father have a lot in common.

Graduation

Ah, college graduation, the point in your life when you say, "Now what?" Or, "Oh shit, now I gotta get a job." I was the first person in my family to get a college degree. My mother was so proud. My dad also attended my graduation, along with his new girlfriend. After the ceremony both my parents congratulated me.

"Ay Michelle, I'm so proud of ju."

"Thanks, Mom."

"I'm proud of you too."

"Thanks, Dad."

My mother gave my father's new girlfriend the evil eye.

"So, Brandon, aren't ju going to introduce us to jur new girlfriend?"

"Uh, yes, of course. Lucy, this is my daughter Michelle and her mother…Carmen."

"It's nice to meet you both."

"So how old are ju, Lucy?"

"I'm thirty-four."

"Thirty-four?"

"Yes."

"Well, ju can be Michelle's older sister."

"Mom, could we not do this now?"

"Do what?"

"This. It was nice to meet you, Lucy. If you'll excuse us, me and my mother have to get going."

Before my mother and I left, my father stopped me.

"Hold on a second, Michelle. I wanted to give you something."

My father handed me a card.

"What is it?"

"Just open it."

Inside the card was a check with a lot of zeros.

"Dad, I can't accept this."

"It's OK. I've been saving it for this day. Use it to get your own apartment."

"My own apartment?"

"Yeah, you don't wanna live at home forever, right?"

"I guess not. Thanks, Dad."

After I finished saying goodbye to my father, my mother and I began to walk to the train station. I began thinking about what my father said. The idea of moving out never occurred to me. Aside from living with Angie I had never been away from my mother, but more importantly I'd never lived on my own. I knew I would move out eventually, but now it seemed so...real.

Moving Out

Today's the day, August 1, 2001. I'm moving out. During the summer, I focused on my acting career. I got my headshots, opened an account with Backstage, and started going to auditions. Some parts I got, some I didn't. At first I auditioned for everything. I needed to build up my résumé.

When I wasn't working on a project, I was spending time with my mother. I felt bad about leaving her. Before I moved out, she taught me how to cook and how to do laundry properly. Apparently, throwing the clothes in the machine and adding soap isn't enough. I also got a job as a waitress, like every other actress in New York City. As far as my apartment was concerned, I wanted to get out of the Bronx. I needed a change, but Manhattan was so damn expensive. That just left Brooklyn and Queens, and you know how I feel about Brooklyn. So like Eddie

Murphy in *Coming to America*, I chose Queens—Astoria to be exact.

On moving day, my father helped me. I didn't take any of the furniture from my room. All of the furniture in my room was very old, plus I wanted a fresh start. I just took all my clothes, books, comics, posters, music CDs, DVDs, and all my personal knickknacks.

Later that day, my father and I arrived at my new apartment. The apartment seemed so big, maybe because it was empty. My new furniture wouldn't arrive until the next day. That night I slept on the floor; well, I slept on a very thick quilt, but the quilt was on the floor. I had trouble sleeping that night. I was so excited to finally be on my own, but I was also scared. I was an adult now. I also missed my mother. I wanted to call her, but it was very late. So I did the next best thing. I parked my ass on my new windowsill, lit up a joint, and gazed at the beautiful, bright moon.

Adulthood

You know, living by yourself really sucks. At first it's great. I arranged my furniture, put my clothes in my new dresser, put my books on my new bookcase, installed blinds and curtains, put up my posters, set up my television and computer desk, and arranged all my knickknacks. When you live by yourself you can walk around naked in your own apartment. Believe it or not when I lived with my mother I couldn't walk around naked. I tried it once when I was sixteen. One night my mother walked in on me while I was naked in the kitchen.

"Michelle, what are ju doing?!"

"I couldn't sleep so I decided to grab a snack."

"Why are ju naked?"

"I dunno, because it's comfortable."

"Put some clothes on, right now!"

"But, Mom, we're the only ones here."

"I don't care. Ju put some clothes on right now!"

"OK, OK."

After that I never walked around naked in the house again, at least not while my mother was home. Anyway, aside from being able to walk around naked in your own apartment, you can throw your clothes on the floor (and leave them there), and you can let the dishes pile up. Not that I'm a slob or anything like that, I'm actually quite neat; it's just that sometimes you get lazy, you know how it is. No one is telling you what to do, or what not to do. You can have your friends over whenever you want, and that's exactly what happened. Every weekend my friends came over, and we smoked weed and drank beer. Well, they drank beer, I'm not much of a beer drinker. But after a while it gets boring, mainly because your friends never clean up after themselves, and they stink up the bathroom.

So the first few months are great, but after that you have to wake up and smell the coffee. That coffee being adulthood—ugh. Now I have to cook for myself, clean up after myself, and do my own laundry. So basically, I have to be responsible. Adulthood really sucks. Another drawback to living alone is coming home to an empty house. I heard horror stories about roommates so I opted not to get a roommate, plus I only had a one-bedroom apartment. So long story short, living alone has its ups and downs, but it's a necessary part of adulthood. Maybe I'll get a cat.

September 11, 2001

I don't think I can say anything about September 11 that hasn't already been said. In May of 2001, I graduated from Lehman College with my bachelor's degree in theater, but as you may know, when you graduate the school doesn't give you your actual diploma during the ceremony. So I went to pick up my diploma on September 11, 2001. I reached the Bedford Avenue stop just after 8:46 a.m. There was a lot of commotion in the train station. I asked someone what happened, and they told me that a plane crashed into the north tower of the World Trade Center. At first no one suspected terrorism, everyone thought it was some sort of freak accident. I was thankful that I didn't know anyone that worked in the World Trade Center, but at the same time I was very sad for the victims of the plane crash, and of course for the people inside the World Trade Center. At that point I wasn't sure what to do. Should I pick up my diploma or should I just go home? Since I was only a block away from the college, I decided to pick up my diploma. Before picking up my diploma, I stopped by the cafeteria to watch the news. That's when I saw it. The north tower was up in smoke. Then at 9:03 a.m. a second plane crashed into the south tower. That's when we knew it wasn't a freak accident, it was terrorism. Nineteen terrorists hijacked four planes. Two hit the World Trade Center, one plane hit the Pentagon, and the final plane crashed on the ground in Shanksville, PA. I just stood there motionless in front of the television, along with hundreds of other students. I couldn't believe this was happening. How could something like this happen in America? I felt vulnerable. Then I saw people jumping from the window. They were trapped. They couldn't reach the elevators, nor could they reach the stairs. Help couldn't reach them, so apart from dying from smoke inhalation, their only other choice was to jump. Every time a jumper landed on the ground there was a loud bang. Seeing them jump was difficult, but hearing them land was even more difficult. At 9:59 a.m. the south tower collapsed. At 10:28 a.m. the north tower collapsed. The terrorist group Al-Qaeda claimed responsibility for the attacks. Almost three thousand people died. At least six thousand were wounded. To this day, it saddens me. Suffice to say, I did not pick up my diploma that day.

Blackout

So guess what happened on August 14, 2003, just after 4:00 p.m.? Another motherfucking blackout, can you believe it? I was on my way home when it happened. I was on the number 5 train headed to 59th Street, where I was supposed to transfer to the N train to Astoria, but suddenly the train stopped, almost as if someone pulled the emergency brake. As the train stopped the lights went out for a few seconds. When the lights came back on they were very dim. The air conditioning also went out. Meanwhile it was ninety degrees that day. A few minutes later the conductor made an announcement:

"Ladies and gentlemen, there has been a city-wide blackout. If power isn't restored, we may have to evacuate the train. I'll update you shortly."

Update you shortly, my ass. Thirty minutes later and still no update. At this point I was pissed off. It was hot, it was the beginning of rush hour, and I was stuck on a jam-packed train with no air conditioning. People were fanning themselves with their magazines. Men started taking off their shirts; shit, even women started taking off their shirts. That's how hot it was. One woman said:

"These motherfuckers can stare at my titties all day, I don't give a shit—it's hot."

In all fairness, she did have some nice titties. Anyway, after a fight almost broke out, I was like, fuck this shit, I'm outta here.

Being that I used to do graffiti, I wasn't afraid to walk in the tunnels. So I walked to the end of the train car, to where the doors connect, I opened the door, and I removed the chains. Just before I was going to jump onto the tracks, someone said:

"What are you doing?"

"I'm getting outta here."

"You're going to walk on the train tracks?"

"Uh, yeah."

"But that's dangerous, what about the third rail?"

"It's a blackout—there's no power."

"But what if the power comes on?"

"I've been on the tracks several times, I'm well aware of the third rail."

Then I jumped onto the train tracks and started walking to 59th Street. Although it was scary, it was also exciting. I hadn't been on the train tracks for over fifteen years. I used my cellphone as a makeshift flashlight. The tunnels were completely empty. No one else was in the tunnels; they hadn't started evacuating people from the trains yet. This would have been the perfect time to go bombing, if I had still been a graffiti writer.

So after walking for about fifteen minutes, I reached 59th Street. I pulled myself up from the train tracks onto the platform, and then I made my way upstairs. The streets were jam-packed with people. Everyone was walking home. All of the traffic lights were out. Not only were the traffic cops directing traffic but regular citizens were directing traffic. People were stuck in elevators, trains, and trams, like the Roosevelt Island tram. All Broadway shows were canceled, the ATMs weren't working, and a lot of stores and restaurants began to close, probably for fear of looting. Taxis were stuffed with passengers; meanwhile many taxis jacked up their rates. While I was crossing the 59th Street Bridge to get to Astoria, I saw a motorcycle with three passengers. The 59th Street Bridge was packed with people trying to make their way home to Queens. It took me two hours to get home—two fucking hours. The blackout didn't only affect New York City; it affected Detroit, Cleveland, Newark, Niagara Falls, Ottawa, Albany, and Norwalk. At first the United States blamed Canada for the blackout—figures. Then they blamed the blackout on lightning. Regardless of whose fault it was, at least it wasn't as bad as the blackout of 1977. You know what they say, shit always happens in threes? Therefore, I predict that there will be at least one more blackout in New York City in my lifetime.

Immigration

The year was 2014. The last few years had been uneventful. I continued to work as a waitress and freelance actress; that's a fancy way of saying I made little or no money as an actress, but I was following my passion, and therefore I was happy. As for girlfriends, they came and left—mostly left. In 2008, I started graduate school at Brooklyn College, and in 2010 I received my master's in acting.

Shortly after, I began teaching full time. I was teaching acting and other theater classes to high school students—no more waitressing, not that there's anything wrong with that. Anyway, in 2014, I had a student by the name of Cynthia Rodriguez. Cynthia was fourteen years old, and she wanted to be an actor. She was my best student. Cynthia was born in the United States but her parents were born in Mexico. Cynthia's mother, Andrea, and her husband, Pablo, came to the United States fourteen years ago. Andrea was still pregnant with Cynthia when she crossed the border. Her goal was to make it to the United States before Cynthia was born; this way Cynthia would automatically become a citizen. And that's exactly what happened. Two days after Andrea and Pablo arrived in the

United States, Cynthia was born. Pablo works in construction, and Andrea works in a restaurant. They have four children. Cynthia is the oldest child. Four years ago, Andrea and Pablo began the process of getting their green cards. Pablo got his green card last year, but Andrea's application has been repeatedly delayed. Now I know what you're thinking, why didn't they apply for green cards sooner? To be honest, I don't know. Maybe they were busy adjusting to life in New York City. Maybe they were busy with work. Maybe they were busy raising their family. Regardless of the reason, they're good people and good parents. So why am I telling you this story? Because two days ago Andrea's restaurant was raided by immigration agents or ICE (Immigration and Customs Enforcement), and since Andrea doesn't have a green card, and since her work permit has expired, she was taken to an immigration facility. Naturally, Cynthia and her family were upset. I went to see them. She told me that her father hired an immigration lawyer, but the immigration lawyer wasn't hopeful about getting Andrea released before she was deported back to Mexico. I told Cynthia and her father that I would help in any way I could. But the truth is I didn't know how to help. I didn't know anything about immigration. So I decided to do some research. I began my research by going to an immigration rally at City Hall. Hundreds of people came to support the rally. Many people spoke at the rally, but one person in particular stood out from the rest. Her name was Gisele Santiago and this is what she had to say about immigration:

"My name is Gisele Santiago, and I'm an immigrant. Immigrant…I don't like that word. Like many before me, I came here illegally. I came here to give my daughter a better life. My daughter, who's in El Salvador with my mother. The United States is a great country with a lot of opportunities, but it's not perfect. I've heard people say horrible things about immigrants such as, 'All immigrants should be shipped back to Mexico, or Guatemala, or wherever the hell they came from. We don't have room for them here. They're taking all our jobs. They come here, and they don't even speak English. They're not American. My family can be traced all the way back to the Pilgrims.' These are just some of the horrible things that some people are saying, and you know what? It's disgusting. The immigrants that come to the United States endure many hardships, all to give their families back home a better life. Every chance I get, I send money to my family in El Salvador. We do the jobs that no one else wants—and we do it for less than minimum wage. I don't know any immigrant that only has one job. I don't know any immigrant that only works eight hours a day. During the weekdays, I work as a waitress, and on the weekends, I work as a maid. I work seven days a week, ten hours a day, sometimes more. I don't get sick time, vacation time, insurance, or a pension. Some people say, 'Well, that's the choice you made when you decided to come here.' It wasn't a choice—a choice is when you're given the option to say yes or no. Coming here was a necessity—a necessity in order to give my daughter a better life. Unless they have something negative to say, most people don't even notice us—we're invisible to the world, yet they need us. We're your cooks, your waitresses, your gardeners, your lawyers, and your teachers—but as long as your food is cooked, and your grass is cut, you don't care. And what does it really mean to be an American? This country was founded by the Pilgrims, yet the Pilgrims came from Great Britain, so if the Pilgrims came from Great Britain, then what does that make them? It makes them immigrants—and they took the land from the Native Americans, who were here first. This country was built with the help of immigrants from all over the world. In my opinion we're all immigrants."

I was very touched by Gisele's words. After hearing Gisele speak I decided that I wanted to see the border wall for myself. So I took a few days off from work and flew out to Nogales, Arizona. When I arrived, I was stunned by the vastness of the wall. It was like we were at war. While there I saw a young girl hugging a woman through the fence. The woman was her mother. Her mother was on the Mexican side of the border. She had been recently deported back to Mexico. I asked if I could speak to her. Her name was Maria Fernandez Rojas.

"Me and my husband came to the United States illegally seven years ago. Six months ago, I was deported back to Mexico. Last week I tried to enter the United States, but I was caught and sent back to Mexico. Now they're telling me that because I tried to enter the country illegally, I can't enter the United States for another five years. I can't be without my daughter for five years. She's nine years old now, soon to be ten. I was trying to make it back in time for her birthday. I came with a group of five and one guide. The guides are supposed to safely take us across the borders, and then to a rest area, where we would be picked up by someone with a van, who would then drop us off at our destination. In my case, it was the bus depot in Nogales. I was planning on taking a bus back to Tucson, but after hiking for two days in the desert I began to tire, and I couldn't keep up. So the guide and the rest of the group left me. I had to pay the guide. Different guides have different prices. I paid two thousand dollars. The drug cartels also smuggle people, but they charge a lot more, it can be anywhere from five to ten thousand dollars. I was afraid to come by myself. Horrible things happen to women that come alone. I've heard stories of women getting robbed, raped, and sometimes even kidnapped. Regardless of the dangers, I have to keep trying. Next time I'll use a different guide. Things are difficult in Mexico. The rich stay rich, and the poor stay poor. As much as I miss my daughter, I'm glad she's in the United States. It's better that I suffer and not her, but still, I want to be with my family. I just want to go home."

After I spoke to Maria I decided to speak to a Border Patrol Agent. I wanted to hear his side of things. His name was John Mitchell.

"I've been protecting our borders for ten years now and I'll tell you something, I've seen it all. Every day thousands of illegal immigrants try to make it into the United States. They come by land, sea, and air. Some walk the desert for days, some swim across on makeshift rafts, some get smuggled in by small planes, cars, or trucks. Once I caught a couple that had three illegal immigrants in their car trunk. Can you imagine, three grown men crammed into a car trunk? Apparently they were in there for four hours. Meanwhile it was 100 degrees outside. Sometimes illegals try to swim across. Some make it, however many don't. Every week Harbor Patrol finds bodies floating in the Rio Grande. Most illegal immigrants pay a guide, or as we call them, a 'coyote,' to help them get into the country. But at the first sign of trouble, the coyote will ditch them in a heartbeat, leaving them stranded in the middle of nowhere. Sometimes people ask me, 'How can you do your job? You're preventing people from getting a better life.' My response to that is that people don't always have all the facts. I would say that 80 to 90 percent of the people we catch are good, hardworking people that just want a better life, but the other 10 to 20 percent are criminals. Aside from illegal immigrants, every day criminals try to smuggle drugs or weapons into this country—and it's our job to stop them. Drug cartels use mules to smuggle their drugs into the country. A mule is a term we use to describe a person that attempts to smuggle drugs into the U.S. The mules walk across the desert carrying makeshift bags filled with drugs, called bundles. Each bundle can weigh anywhere from fifty to one hundred pounds. The really sad cases are when we encounter human smugglers. They swallow the drugs for transport. Once I had a sixteen-year-old girl who swallowed two pounds of cocaine, but something went wrong, two of the bags broke, and the girl died. Apparently, she had an arrangement with the drug dealer: she transports the drugs and in exchange gets free transportation to the United States. That's how badly people want to get into this country. I'm sympathetic to the people that are trying to come here for a better life, but despite that, I have a job to do, and I intend to do it."

Before I returned home, I spoke to an immigration lawyer. I wanted see what was required in order to get a green card, and I wanted to hear his views on immigration.

"What is America? It's the land of opportunity. People come here for a better life. It's been the land of opportunity since the Pilgrims came here. I'm not saying that we should just open our doors to everyone. If we did that the United States would become overpopulated. What I am saying is, we need to know where we came from, we need to know our history, and we need to understand why people want to come here. The reality is that this country was built by immigrants—and immigrants are still building this country. I mean, take a look around. Immigrants are everywhere, and the majority of people don't care. When you're eating in a restaurant and an immigrant waitress brings you your food, do you care? No, the only thing you care about is that your food tastes good. When you're staying in a hotel, do you care that an immigrant is making your bed while you're gone? No, you don't, you're just happy that you didn't have to make it yourself. The immigrants that come here make great sacrifices, and it's my job as an immigration lawyer to make sure that those sacrifices aren't in vain. So what's the process for applying for a green card? Well, if someone wants to apply for a green card through their family, they have to fill out an I-130, which costs 420. If they want to apply for a green card through their job, they have to fill out an I-140, which costs 580. If you want to apply for a permanent residency, then you have to fill out an I-485, which costs 985, plus biometrics which cost 85. Biometrics is fingerprinting. And if you want to renew your green card you have to fill out an I-90 which is 365, plus 85 for biometrics. And just because a person applies for a green card doesn't mean they'll get accepted, and every time you apply, you have to pay the fee again. So what does all this tell you? That applying for a green card is expensive and time consuming. And the worst part is, while you're waiting for your paperwork to go through, you can still be deported. I've heard people say, 'Why don't immigrants use their money to come here legally?' Why? Because it takes years to come here legally, and when you're living in poverty, and surrounded by violence, years are too long. I don't condone coming here illegally, it's dangerous and of course it's illegal, but I understand why people do it. And if I were in their shoes, I would probably come here illegally too."

The following day I returned home. I immediately went to see Cynthia and her family. Turns out Andrea was deported back to Mexico that morning. What kind of country do we live in where we tear families apart? I also asked myself, what does it mean to be an American? In a country that was built by immigrants—in a country that was founded by immigrants, how can anyone be illegal? Can you imagine what would happen if all the immigrants in the United States decided not to come to work tomorrow? That's how much of an impact they have on our economy and our society. We need them and they need us. From now on, I choose to be a voice for anyone who is coming here for a better life. A voice for the people that we call "illegal immigrants" or "illegal aliens." What we should be calling them is "human beings."

Transgender

So I have to admit, I don't entirely understand transgender people. For example, let's say a man becomes a woman, he starts taking hormones, gets breast implants, and surgically has his penis removed. Now he's a transgender woman, but this transgender woman doesn't menstruate or have a uterus, and can't experience childbirth. So biologically, this transgender woman isn't really a woman. Now don't get me wrong, I support transgender rights, and I think all transgender people should be treated equally, but changing your sex just seems so…invasive.

So why I am discussing transgender? Well, my cousin Alejandro called me and wanted to talk. Everyone in the family has always suspected that Alejandro is gay but he's always denied it. Alejandro had just turned eighteen and was going to start college in the fall. He wanted to become a costume designer. We met at a restaurant and talked.

"Thanks for seeing me, Michelle."

"No problem. So what did you want to talk to me about?"

"You know, it's always been easy for me to talk to you, Michelle. Maybe it's because you're gay, or maybe it's because you're so down to earth, but either way there's something I need to get off my chest, and I feel like you're the only person who will understand."

"You can tell me anything, Alejandro."

"So I know everyone thinks I'm gay, but I'm not."

"Is that what you wanted to tell me?"

"No. OK, so I'm just going to spit it out. I want to be a woman."

"You wanna be a woman?"

"Yes."

"So you wanna have a sex change?"

"Yes. You don't approve?"

"What makes you say that?"

"Well, for starters you have that 'I don't approve' look on your face."

"Alejandro, it's not that I don't approve. It's just that I don't understand why."

"I figured if anyone would understand, it would be you."

"Why would I understand?"

"Because you're gay."

"So being gay and being transgender are completely different. Just because I like vagina doesn't mean I want a penis—although it would make peeing in public bathrooms a lot easier—but anyway, let me ask you this, do you like men?"

"Yes."

104

"So, you're gay?"

"No, it's because I'm a woman."

"You're a woman?"

"Yes, on the inside."

"I'm confused."

"Ugh, it's hard to explain."

"Try."

"For as long as I can remember I've always had this feeling inside me, this feeling of being trapped, trapped in the wrong body, and when I put on women's clothes and makeup, that feeling goes away."

"Maybe you're a—"

"I'm not a transvestite! I just feel like I was born in the wrong body."

"OK. So let's say you go through with it, you become a woman. How are you going to pay for the sex change?"

"I would use my college fund."

"If you use your college fund, how will you pay for college?"

"I'll get a job. I'll get a loan. I don't know, but I'll figure it out."

"Have you discussed this with your parents?"

"Of course not. If I do they'll probably throw me out."

"So you were just gonna show up to your house as a woman one day?"

"I guess, I dunno."

"Alejandro, I don't think you should do this."

"Michelle, I'm miserable in this body. I'm sad. I'm depressed. Every day it's a struggle to go on. I've wanted to be a woman since I was six years old. I can't keep it in anymore. It's just that I feel like I'm a woman on the inside, you know…in my soul."

I was moved by Alejandro's words. I sat there quietly for a moment and thought about what he said.

"OK. I'll support you."

"Thank you."

"But you have to tell your parents first."

"Will you come with me?"

"Of course."

Suffice to say Alejandro's parents didn't take the news well, and in fact he was right, they threw him out. I told Alejandro he could stay with me, but he said he was going to stay with a friend. It reminded me of when Carlos's parents threw him out and abandoned him. Little by little Alejandro started the process of becoming a woman. A year later he was a full-blown woman. He changed his name to Julia after his favorite actress, Julia Roberts. I have to say Julia is one sexy bitch. Anyway, I hope Julia's parents accept her one day. Because of Julia I now have a better understanding of what it means to be transgender.

Cancer, Part One

On September 1, 2016, I went to visit my mother. While I was talking to my mother about work, she appeared light-headed.

"Mom, are you OK?"

"Jes, I'm fine."

"You look a little pale."

"I said, I'm—"

Suddenly, she passed out.

"Mom! Mom!"

She didn't respond. I called 911. Just before the paramedics came, my mother woke up. Being the stubborn woman that my mother is, she didn't want to go the hospital, but I insisted that she go to the hospital and get evaluated. While my mother was waiting in the emergency room the doctor came in.

"Ms. Perez?"

"Jes."

"Hi. I'm Dr. Cervantes, it's nice to meet you."

"It's nice to meet ju too. This is my daughter, Michelle."

"Nice to meet you, Dr. Cervantes."

"Likewise. So, Ms. Perez, I understand you passed out?"

"Jes."

"For how long?"

"Just for a few seconds."

"Have you been sick lately?"

"No."

"Any weakness?"

"Jes."

"For how long?"

"A few months, off and on."

"Aside from the weakness has anything else been going on?"

My mother looked at me for a moment before answering.

"Well...jes."

"What is it?"

"I have a...lump on my left breast."

"How long have you had it?"

"For about ten months."

I was shocked and angry.

"Ten months, Mom? You've had a lump on your breast for ten months and you didn't tell me anything?"

"I didn't want ju to worry."

"What the hell is wrong with you?"

"Watch jur mouth!"

"I will not watch my mouth!"

Dr. Cervantes stepped in.

"Ladies, ladies, ladies, perhaps you can finish this conversation later...in private."

My mother and I apologized.

"OK. So I'm going to have the nurse draw some blood. As for the lump on your left breast, I'm going to refer you to an oncologist. Do you have any questions, Ms. Perez?"

"No."

The results from the blood work showed that my mother's blood count was very low, which could be indicative of cancer, but further testing was needed, so Dr. Cervantes referred my mother to an oncologist. Soon after, my mother was discharged. Later that day, when we arrived at my mother's house, we continued our conversation.

"So…are you ready to talk?"

"Talk about what?"

"Talk about how you had a lump on your breast for ten months without telling me—without telling anyone."

"Ay no, I don't want to talk about that."

"Mom, you know what this means, right?"

"Jes, I know."

"Then why didn't you say anything? Why didn't you do anything?"

"I don't know, Michelle. Maybe I was scared. Maybe I was in denial. What difference does it make now?"

"Mom, it's OK to feel that way. It's just that…I'm worried about you, that's all."

"I know, mija. Now ju better go home, I'm going to bed early tonight."

"No, I'm staying over."

"Fine, but if ju get up during the middle of the night to grab a snack make sure ju put some clothes on. I don't wanna catch you naked in the kitchen."

"Yes, Mother."

Cancer, Part Two

The next day my mother made an appointment to see an oncologist. Her appointment was in two weeks. I went with my mother to see the oncologist. The oncologist examined the lump on my mother's left breast and she checked for additional lumps.

After the examination, the oncologist made an appointment for my mother to get a mammogram, and she ordered a biopsy of the lump on her breast. The biopsy tested positive for cancer. My mother had stage-four breast cancer. The oncologist had to work fast. So my mother began chemotherapy. I knew about the side effects of chemotherapy, so I decided to stay with my mother until she was well again. The chemotherapy made her very sick. First there was nausea and vomiting. Then there was dehydration caused by the nausea and vomiting. Then there was extreme weakness caused by the dehydration. My mother also lost her appetite. And if that wasn't enough, her hair began to fall out. That was very hard for my mother. My mother had long black hair. She was very proud of her hair. She never cut it, never. Within a month, she was bald. I offered to buy her a wig but she refused. She just wore a scarf over her head. Then the depression began. I didn't know what to do. Every day someone from the family would come to visit my mother in an attempt to raise her spirits, but regardless of who came to visit it didn't help. So I decided to call my father. He came to see my mother right away.

"How long has she been sick?"

"About a month?"

"Why didn't you call me sooner?"

"I figured you were busy with your third wife and all?"

"Lucy divorced me two months ago."

"Let me guess, she got tired of you cheating on her?"

My father gave me a stern look.

"Where is your mother now?"

"In the living room."

My father entered the living room. My mother was seated in her rocking chair. The sun was coming down. As the light from the sunset broke through the window, striking my mother, it seemed to give her face a warm glow. My father approached her.

"Carmen."

"Brandon, what are ju doing here?"

"I came to see you."

"Shouldn't ju be with jur wife, la sucia?"

"I'm not with Lucy anymore."

"Oh. What happened, did she fall down the stairs, or get hit by a city bus?"

"No."

"Oh well, that's too bad."

"Do you need anything?"

"Jes, I need some new tetas, these have cancer."

"I can't help you with that but perhaps I make you something to eat?"

"Something to eat? Ju don't know how to cook."

"I learned."

"Ju learned how to cook, since when?"

"Since recently."

"Are ju any good?"

"I still have a lot to learn but I'm getting there."

"What can ju cook?"

"Not much, rice, beans, chicken, and roasted vegetables."

"Since when do you eat roasted vegetables?"

"The doctor said my blood pressure is high so I'm trying to eat healthy. So no more fried eggs with bacon and cheese, no more fast food, no more red meat, and I even started eating brown rice instead of white or yellow."

"Hmph. Ok, make me some roasted vegetables and chicken—but I'm warning ju, if it doesn't taste good, I'm not eating it."

"Fair enough."

So my father cooked and my mother ate. Of course she gave my father a lot of critiques. From then on, my father came to see my mother every day. He spent hours with her. They gossiped about friends and family and talked about Puerto Rico. He lifted her spirits. Her health seemed to be improving, or so we thought.

Cancer, Part Three

Although my mother's spirits were improving, her health wasn't; the cancer got worse. So my mother was admitted to the hospital. One day after work I went to the hospital to visit my mother. As I was walking to the hospital entrance I heard someone call my name.

"Michelle!"

It was Jessica Hernandez. She walked over to me.

"Hey, Michelle, how are you?"

"I'm OK. How are you?"

"I'm good."

"What brings you here?"

"I was visiting my partner from work, he's got appendicitis. What about you, what brings you here?"

"My mother was admitted to the hospital."

"Is she OK?"

"Breast cancer."

"Oh, I'm sorry."

"Thanks. Look, I gotta get going."

"OK, listen, if you ever wanna talk, maybe over drinks, here's my number."

"Talk?"

"Yes."

"Over drinks?"

"Yeah."

"Like a date?"

"Well, I try not to use labels."

"Are you gay?"

"Yes."

"Wow, my gaydar must be broken. But anyway, uh, yeah, maybe after my mother gets better we can…talk."

"Sure, I hope your mother feels better."

"Thanks."

So I took Jessica's number and then I went upstairs to see my mother. When I entered my mother's room she was sleeping. She looked very peaceful. I didn't want to wake her, but I was worried about her.

"Mom."

"Jes."

"Are you OK?"

"Jes…just tired."

"Where's Dad, I thought he was here?"

"I sent him to get me some real food, hospital food is horrible."

"Did the doctor say anything about the cancer?"

"We can talk about that later. First I have a question for ju."

"What is it?"

"Are ju seeing anyone?"

"What?"

"Do ju have a girlfriend?"

"What kind of question is that?"

"Just answer the question."

"No, I don't have a girlfriend."

"Have ju gone on any dates?"

"Well, I went on a date two months ago with a nurse but it didn't go well."

"A nurse?

"Yes."

"Nurses make good money. Is she Puerto Rican?"

"No, she's not Puerto Rican."

"Is she black?"

"What difference does that make?"

"I'm just curious, is she black?"

"Yes, she's black."

"Can't ju find jurself a nice Puerto Rican girl?"

"You see, this is why I didn't tell you. You have a problem with black people."

"I do not have a problem with black people."

"Yes, you do."

"I have black friends."

"People who have problems with black people always say that."

"Michelle, I don't have any problems with black people. Now, where does this nurse work?"

"Actually, she works in this hospital."

"Really? Does she work on this floor?"

"No, she works in the emergency room."

"Can she get me free TV?"

"Mom, we only had one date. I can't ask her to get you free TV."

"Ju can try—and when are ju going to have kids?"

"I dunno."

"Well ju better hurry up, ju're not getting any younger. Are ju going to adopt or do that inverto whatever?"

"In-vitro fertilization."

"How does it work again?"

"They take a man's sperm and insert it into a woman's egg."

"Well ju just make sure the sperm is Puerto Rican."

"Mom, why are you so concerned with my love life?"

"I'm worried about ju. I don't want ju to be alone."

"Why are you concerned about me being alone? Mom, what did the doctor say?"

"The cancer has spread."

"Where has it spread to?"

"To my liver and other parts of my body."

"OK, so what does that mean?"

"It means I'm dying, Michelle."

"Dying? You can't be dying. Can't they get rid of the cancer? I mean, there's radiation—there's surgery. Can't they do a liver transplant or something?"

"No, Michelle, they can't."

"But you don't look so bad."

"Michelle, ju have to accept it."

"No, I won't accept it!"

"Ju have to! I'm sorry, Michelle. I waited too long. You were right. I should have gone to the doctor sooner. Now we have to start preparing."

Then I hugged my mother like I never hugged her before. I cried in her arms. Soon after, my father walked in.

"I got lunch."

My father saw that I had been crying. He asked:

"Is everything OK?"

My mother hadn't told my father yet. After my mother told my father he just stayed quiet for a moment, then he said:

"Carmen, there's something I have to ask you."

"What is it?"

"I was going to wait until you got better but considering…"

"What is it, Brandon?"

"Will you marry me?"

"Marry ju?"

"Yes. You're the only woman I ever truly loved."

"Well…I just have one question."

"What is it?"

"Where's my ring?"

"It's in my apartment. I can bring it tomorrow."

"No, ju can bring it today."

"So is that a yes?"

"Jes, I'll marry you."

So my parents remarried a few days later. My mother's room was packed with family and friends. She was so happy. Two weeks later my mother died. It was November 15, 2016. That's when I realized it. I hate cancer. I really, really fucking hate cancer.

Farewell

A few days after my mother's funeral, I went to her apartment. As for my mother's belongings, my father and I agreed to donate everything to the Salvation Army except for my mother's photos and personal knickknacks. I began putting everything in boxes. When the Salvation Army arrived, they took everything except my mother's rocking chair. I just couldn't part with it. Before I left I took one last look at the apartment. I spent most of my life here; however, without my mother the apartment just felt so…empty. That night I couldn't sleep. I still couldn't believe that my mother was gone. I got up from bed and walked over to my mirror. I looked at myself for a few moments, then I grabbed a pair of scissors and I began cutting my hair. It was like I was in a trance or something. I just kept cutting and cutting. Maybe I was sad over my mother's death, maybe I was angry, maybe I was making a statement since my mother died from cancer, or maybe I just felt it was time for a change. Regardless of the reason, cutting my hair made me feel better.

2016

The year was 2016. *Rogue One: A Star Wars Story* came out. "We have hope. Rebellions were built on hope." I have to say, it was really good—way better than those other prequels, you know, the ones George Lucas directed. Oh George, what were you thinking? Another great movie that came out was *The Lobster*, starring Colin Farrell. "Now have you thought of what animal you'd like to be if you end up alone?" Also *Captain America: Civil War* came out. The best part about the movie was that Spider-Man was in it—woo-hoo. "When you can do the things that I can, but you don't and then the bad things happen, they happen because of you."

2016 was also a good year for songs. There was "Hello" by Adele. "Hello, it's me. I was wondering if after all these years you'd like to meet. To go over everything. They say that time's supposed to heal ya. But I ain't done much healing." Then there was "Don't Wanna Know" by Maroon 5. "I don't wanna know, know, know, know. Who's taking you home, home, home, home. And lovin' you so, so, so, so. The way I used to love ya, no." Last but not least there was "Cake by the Ocean" by DNCE. "Ay, ya, ya, ya, ya. I keep on hopin' we'll eat cake by the ocean."

As for the Yankees, they didn't win the World Series, but at least there weren't any blackouts. Caitlyn Jenner—the athlete formerly known as Bruce Jenner—was on the cover of Sports Illustrated.

As for me, well, I'm thirty-nine years old, and I'm single with no kids. I do have a date next week with Jessica. That's right, I'm going on a date with my bully from elementary school, who's now a police officer. I wonder if she'll bring her handcuffs. Anyway, apart from being thirty-nine and single, and apart from being a full-time teacher, I'm still a struggling actress—struggling but not starving.

So I guess my story has come to an end. I'm afraid I don't have any mind-blowing advice for you. Life is hard, shit, life fucking sucks. But life can be great too. I guess you have to take the good with the bad. God knows I've had my ups and downs, but I got through it. In the end, it made me a stronger person. Anyway, I hope you learned something. I know I did.